TERRIER IN THE TINSEL

Mandy went down the corridor and out the hospital's main doors. She was just going to walk across the parking lot when she stopped in her tracks.

A small brown-and-white Jack Russell terrier was standing a short distance away, watching her.

"Hello," she said gently. "What are you doing here, all on your own?"

The little dog whined softly. But although it wagged its long tail, it didn't come any nearer.

The little dog looked at her with intelligent brown eyes but stood its ground. Then its ears twitched, and for a moment, Mandy's spirits lifted. It was going to come to her!

Suddenly, the dog gave another soft whine, then turned and dashed away into some shrubs.

Read all the Animal Ark books!

Where animals come first ®

by Ben M. Baglio

$3.99 US Each!

- ❏ BDB 0-439-09700-2 **Bunnies in the Bathroom**
- ❏ BDB 0-439-34407-7 **Cat in a Crypt**
- ❏ BDB 0-439-34393-3 **Cats at the Campground**
- ❏ BDB 0-439-34413-1 **Colt in the Cave**
- ❏ BDB 0-439-34386-0 **Dog at the Door**
- ❏ BDB 0-439-34408-5 **Dog in the Dungeon**
- ❏ BDB 0-439-23021-7 **Dolphin in the Deep**
- ❏ BDB 0-439-34415-8 **Foal in the Fog**
- ❏ BDB 0-439-34385-2 **Foals in the Field**
- ❏ BDB 0-439-23018-7 **Guinea Pig in the Garage**
- ❏ BDB 0-439-09701-0 **Hamster in a Handbasket**
- ❏ BDB 0-439-34387-9 **Horse in the House**
- ❏ BDB 0-439-44891-3 **Hound at the Hospital**
- ❏ BDB 0-439-44897-2 **Hound on the Heath**

- ❏ BDB 0-439-09698-7 **Kitten in the Cold**
- ❏ BDB 0-590-18749-X **Kittens in the Kitchen**
- ❏ BDB 0-439-34392-5 **Mare in the Meadow**
- ❏ BDB 0-590-66231-7 **Ponies at the Point**
- ❏ BDB 0-439-34388-7 **Pony in a Package**
- ❏ BDB 0-590-18750-3 **Pony on the Porch**
- ❏ BDB 0-439-34391-7 **Pup at the Palace**
- ❏ BDB 0-590-18751-1 **Puppies in the Pantry**
- ❏ BDB 0-439-34389-5 **Puppy in a Puddle**
- ❏ BDB 0-590-18757-0 **Sheepdog in the Snow**
- ❏ BDB 0-439-34126-4 **Stallion in the Storm**
- ❏ BDB 0-439-34390-9 **Tabby in the Tub**

Available wherever you buy books, or use this order form.

Scholastic Inc., P.O. Box 7502, Jefferson City, MO 65102

Please send me the books I have checked above. I am enclosing $_____ (please add $2.00 to cover shipping and handling). Send check or money order—no cash or C.O.D.s please.

Name _____Age_____

Address _____

City _____State/Zip _____

Please allow four to six weeks for delivery. Offer good in the U.S. only. Sorry, mail orders are not available to residents of Canada. Prices subject to change.

ANIMAL ARK®

Terrier in the Tinsel

Ben M. Baglio

Illustrations by Jenny Gregory

AN
APPLE
PAPERBACK

SCHOLASTIC INC.

New York Toronto London Auckland Sydney
Mexico City New Delhi Hong Kong Buenos Aires

Special thanks to Sue Bentley

ISBN 0-439-44892-1

14 13 12 11

4 5 6 7 8 9/0

Printed in the U.S.A.

40

One

Mandy Hope walked into the kitchen at Animal Ark. "Dad, what on earth are you doing?" she said, trying not to laugh.

"Hello, dear." Adam Hope smiled as he struggled into the bright red jacket of a Santa suit. "I'm just trying on my costume for the Santaland at Walton Cottage Hospital," he explained.

"Looks to me like it's not going to button! Maybe you should have tried it on before lunch!" Mandy said. "Here, let me help you." She pulled the sides of the jacket together and fastened the buttons. The material strained under the pressure.

1

"Thanks, Mandy," Dr. Adam said with a grin. "This suit must have shrunk when your mom washed it."

"Hmm." Mandy wasn't convinced. "Maybe you should have stuck to your diet!" She laughed.

Dr. Adam flexed his shoulders and looked down at himself. "Nope, this is fine," he insisted. "I'll really look the part." He took off the jacket and hung it on the back of the kitchen door.

"Well, you'll certainly be a perfect Santa, with your round stomach," Mandy teased.

"Smart aleck! Phew, I think we need a cup of tea after that," her dad announced, with an amused gleam in his eye. "I'll make one for your mom, too. She's just finishing up in the operating room."

Mandy remembered that this morning her mom had been operating on Peaches, an elderly guinea pig. Peaches was pretty, with rosettes of creamy fur. She belonged to seven-year-old Laura, who lived near Mandy's best friend, James Hunter.

Emily Hope came into the kitchen just as her husband was filling the kettle. She smiled when she saw Mandy. "No more school till next year!" she joked.

Mandy nodded. "Yup! And I can't wait for Christmas Day. Only four days to go! How's Peaches?"

"She's just come out of the anesthesia," said Dr.

Emily. "She's still pretty groggy. I had to remove a very large gallstone."

"But she's going to pull through, isn't she?" Mandy asked, worried. She knew how much Laura loved her pet.

"It's too early to say, dear," her mom replied, looking serious. She ran a hand through her long red hair. "Peaches is stable at the moment, but we have to remember that she's fairly old."

Mandy nodded. She knew that an operation placed a serious strain on any animal — even more if the animal was getting old. It looked like the next few days were going to be touch-and-go for poor Peaches.

"Maybe Mandy could keep an eye on Peaches," Dr. Adam suggested.

Mandy brightened. She felt better knowing that there was something she could do. "What's that stuff that causes gallstones? Ox-something, acid, isn't it?" she asked.

"That's right. Oxalic acid," her mom replied.

"Caused by eating too many brassicas," Dr. Adam said. He handed Mandy and her mom each a mug of tea.

"What are brassicas?" Mandy asked, taking a cautious sip.

"It's the name for all the plants of the cabbage family," Dr. Emily explained. "Like kale, cauliflower, and spinach. Too much of that kind of food can upset certain guinea pigs."

"So will Peaches need to be put on a special diet when she's better?" Mandy asked.

"Yes. She'll probably do better if she sticks to grass, hay, and grain, with fruit and vegetables in small amounts," Dr. Emily said. "I'll talk with Laura and her mom about it when they phone."

Mandy took her tea over to the window and saw James stepping out of his father's car. "Here's James," she said. "I'd better go get ready. We're going over to Lilac Cottage. Gran and Grandpa will be waiting for us."

"Oh, you're helping to decorate my Santaland at Walton Hospital this afternoon, aren't you?" her dad remembered. "Tell your grandmother that the Santa suit is a perfect fit. And Santa is polishing his boots and grooming his reindeer!"

"Da-ad!" Mandy put her empty mug in the sink and headed for the stairs.

It was cold and frosty in the pale afternoon sun, and Mandy's and James's breath steamed in the air as they walked along the road. Behind the hedge, the fields were bare and bleak.

James lifted his head and sniffed the cold air. "My dad says he can smell snow in the air. But I can't!"

"Me, neither," Mandy said. "I wish it *would* snow. I'd really love a white Christmas."

"Yeah!" James agreed. "Snowball fights and sledding and snowboarding. Blackie loves going for walks in the snow, too." Blackie was James's pet Labrador.

"Blackie loves walks, period!" Mandy said.

James grinned and pushed his glasses up to the bridge of his nose. "He's getting better about walking on a leash, you know," he said proudly. "And he actually came when I called him yesterday."

"Will wonders never cease!" Mandy said affectionately. Blackie was great, but he wasn't exactly obedient.

They had almost reached Lilac Cottage. "Oh, look," Mandy said, waving. "There's Grandpa in the driveway. He's loading up the camper."

Grandpa waved back. "Hello, you two!" he called out as Mandy and James stopped to open the gate. "I'm glad you're here. Just look at this!"

Mandy saw that a pile of wood and some boards were already stacked inside the back of the van. "Are we going to need all that, Grandpa?" she asked.

"Oh, yes. We have to make the framework first, then we decorate it," her grandpa replied.

Dorothy Hope came out of the cottage, her arms full of more props. "Hello, Mandy dear. Hello, James," she called out, peering at them from behind the pile of boxes she was carrying. "This isn't the half of it!" Suddenly, the boxes began to slip sideways. "Oops." Gran gasped.

James dashed over to help. "I've got them!" he said, steadying the load.

"Oh, thank you, dear," Mrs. Hope said gratefully. "There are more boxes in the hallway if you two could get them for me."

Mandy and James helped load all the boxes, which were bulging with decorations, into the van. It was a squeeze to get the back door locked, but Grandpa finally managed it.

"Phew!" James said.

Grandpa chuckled. "Mrs. Ponsonby has been collecting donations of props and decorations for us," he explained. "I've never seen so much tinsel in my life!"

"Mrs. Ponsonby can be very . . . enthusiastic!" Gran opened the door and got into the driver's seat.

"Enthusiastic? That's one word for it," Grandpa murmured.

Mandy and James laughed. Mrs. Ponsonby was the bossiest woman in Welford.

"I bet no one dared to refuse her!" Mandy said.

They drove through the village and took the winding road that led across the moors to Walton. Gran turned on the radio, and a woman's voice filled the van. "So come along, one and all, and bring your gifts to Walton Cottage Hospital."

"Listen! It's the local radio station's Christmas toy drive," Mandy said.

"That's right," said James. "People are being asked to buy an extra Christmas present for the children who will be in the hospital over Christmas. My mom bought one last week."

"Did she? Well, it's for a very good cause," Gran said. "We're going to put a collection box for the gifts in our Santaland. Then Santa will give them out on Christmas Eve."

"Local children can visit Santa there, too," Grandpa added. "We're going to charge them fifty cents a visit and donate the money to the hospital."

Mandy thought that was a great idea.

The stone cottages and farm buildings on the high moors sped past, and soon Gran was turning into the hospital parking lot. She pulled into an empty space near the entrance and turned off the engine. "OK. Let's go and find out where we're supposed to set up," she said.

"I'll go ask," Grandpa volunteered. He undid his seat

belt and climbed out of the van. "I'll only be a minute," he said, walking off.

"Shall we start getting the stuff out, Gran?" Mandy offered.

"Good idea, Mandy." Gran nodded.

By the time Tom Hope returned, they had most of the boxes and all of the wood stacked in the parking lot. "I hadn't realized how much stuff we had." He chuckled, eyeing the impressive pile. "We're in a side room, just down the hall from the children's ward. Straight through the main doors and turn right," he said.

"OK." Mandy and James sprang into action, each grabbing a box of decorations.

They were just returning to the van for a second load when a hospital aide came out of the building. "Hi! I saw you struggling. Need an extra hand?" he asked.

"Oh, thanks," Mandy and James said gratefully.

"No problem," the man replied with a friendly grin, shouldering some of the wood.

In the side room, they found Gran standing with her hands on her hips. Mandy saw that she was looking worriedly at the floor, which was fast disappearing beneath all the material for the Santaland.

"Oh, dear. It looks a little chaotic," Gran said, surveying the mess.

"Perhaps we could start and leave the rest outside for later?" Mandy suggested.

"That's a good idea," James agreed.

"If there's nothing else to bring in for the moment, I'll get back to work," the aide said cheerily. "Bye. Have fun!"

"Thanks for your help!" Mandy called after him.

"Er . . . I suppose there's a plan, Dorothy?" Tom Hope said to his wife.

"Oh, yes. Where's that drawing I made?" Gran produced a piece of paper from her pants pocket. "Here it is." She smoothed it out and laid it on a table at the side of the room.

Mandy, James, and Grandpa studied Gran's drawing. Then they turned back and looked at all the material.

"What are those panel things?" James asked.

"Those are display boards," Gran said, "from a shop that was closing. Mrs. Ponsonby went in and asked if we could have them, since they were just going to throw them away."

"Good for her!" Mandy whispered to James.

Grandpa frowned. "Display boards? They look complicated to me."

"It's pretty easy to put them together," Gran said confidently. "Mandy and James can help me sort through all the parts. Why don't you get your toolbox? We'll need screws and a screwdriver."

"Right," said Grandpa, looking a little happier now that he knew what had to be done. He set off down the hall, whistling under his breath.

"Your grandmother's a brilliant organizer," James whispered.

Mandy grinned. "I know!"

Half an hour later, everything had begun to take shape. The wooden frames for the display boards had been fastened together. Mandy, James, and Gran were steadying the panels while Grandpa slotted them into place.

Mandy caught a movement out of the corner of her eye and looked up. She saw a blond boy looking at them curiously. He looked about nine years old and was wearing a plaid robe over bright yellow pajamas.

Mandy smiled at him, and he flashed her a grin before wandering away.

"Well, what do you think, Dorothy?" Grandpa tightened the final screw.

They all stood back and looked at the display units. There were five of them, each about a yard and a half tall.

"They aren't going to fall over on anybody, are they?" Gran asked, sounding worried.

Grandpa puffed out his chest. "Steady as a rock."

"Gran's just teasing," Mandy said. "I think they're great. Don't you, James?"

"Definitely," James agreed.

Grandpa looked pleased. He turned to his wife. "They'll need to be decorated. The fabric covering the boards is pretty shabby."

"Don't worry," said Gran. "I've got lots of silver wrapping paper, which will be just perfect."

"What are those for?" asked a voice behind Mandy and James.

Mandy turned around. It was the boy who had been watching them earlier. He stood in the doorway, an interested expression on his round face.

"Hi," said Mandy. "We're building a Santaland. I'm Mandy, and this is James," she added. "And that's my gran and grandpa over there. What's your name?"

"Charlie," the little boy replied. "What's it for?"

Mandy explained that it was where local children could visit Santa.

"And children who are in the hospital, like you, can come here, too, or Santa will visit them in the ward," James put in.

Charlie put his head to one side as if he was thinking about this. "I don't need Santa to visit me in bed. I've had bronchitis, but I'm almost better now."

"Oh, that's good," Mandy said. "So you'll be going home for Christmas."

Charlie nodded. "I can't wait. There's not much to do around here. It's really boring."

"We're just about ready to start covering the display boards with silver wrapping paper. Would you like to help us?" Mandy suggested.

"Cool!" Charlie's blue eyes lit up, and he nodded eagerly. He began rummaging around in the nearest box.

While Mandy and James dragged the display boards into position, Charlie pulled out rolls of silver and colored wrapping paper. He heaped them all together on the floor, along with silver streamers and stars, then went to get the rest of the boxes from the hallway.

James was searching for a roll of tape when Charlie suddenly burst through the door and bumped into him.

"Ooh, sorry," Charlie said apologetically, his arms around a large box.

"That's OK." James rubbed his sore ankle.

Mandy gave him a sympathetic look. "Do you have some tape in your toolbox, Grandpa?" she asked, turning to Tom Hope.

"I'm sure I do. Oh, that's funny." Grandpa scratched his head, looking puzzled. "Where *is* my toolbox? It was here just a minute ago."

"It can't be far away, Tom," Gran said. "You just had it."

Mandy and James started looking for the toolbox. But after a couple of minutes they had still found no sign of it.

"That's weird," James said, pushing his hair out of his eyes. "Maybe it's been covered up by something."

He began looking under the coils of streamers and moving empty cardboard boxes. Mandy helped him but had no luck.

"Found it!" Charlie suddenly called out triumphantly. "It was under all this tinsel stuff! Sorry!"

"Mystery solved!" Grandpa said with a grin. He tossed the roll of tape across to James.

James caught it. "I don't know if Charlie's helping or getting in the way," he whispered to Mandy.

"Well, at least he seems to be enjoying himself!" she said with a grin.

"Charlie Kingston!" called a cheery voice from the hall. Then a nurse stuck her head into the room. "Ah, there you are. Your snack is ready in the ward."

Charlie scrunched up his nose. "I don't want it. I want to stay here and help."

"Did someone say snack?" Grandpa said hopefully.

The nurse smiled at him. "I'll see what can be arranged. It's the least we can do for our volunteers! Come along, Charlie, you need to eat something."

"Can't I help here?" Charlie pleaded, his expression downcast.

"You can come back and help later, Charlie," the nurse said.

"We're going to be here for ages, aren't we, Gran?" Mandy asked, seeing Charlie's disappointed face.

"Oh, yes. Probably tomorrow, too," Gran agreed.

"OK." Charlie's face brightened. "I suppose I *am* a little hungry," he said, following the nurse out of the room.

"He's really eager to help, isn't he?" James said. "Imagine being willing to skip your snack!"

"Can't understand that at all!" Mandy replied innocently, opening her eyes wide. James was famous for his healthy appetite.

James blushed a little and grinned at Mandy.

"Here's our snack now," Grandpa said as a nurse came into the room carrying a tray with four cups and a plate of cookies on it. "Thanks. Chocolate chip, my favorite."

James and Mandy perched on the side table and helped themselves.

"I think I'll just run along to see Percy Green in Ward Twelve before we start again," Gran said when she had finished her cup of tea.

"Who's Percy Green?" asked Mandy.

"A recent addition to your gran's meals-on-wheels round," Grandpa said. "The old gentleman was brought in yesterday after a bad asthma attack, wasn't he, Dorothy?"

Gran nodded. "That's right. He collapsed in his yard. Luckily, a neighbor found him and called an ambulance. I'd just like to check up on him."

"I'll come with you," Mandy offered.

"All right," said Gran. "You can help me cheer Percy up. I haven't known him all that long, but I'm sure he'd like some visitors."

Ward Twelve was just down the hall. It was a bright, airy room, made cheerful by the vases of flowers beside most of the beds. Gran checked with the nurse that it was all right to visit Percy.

"Go ahead," the nurse said. "Mr. Green might enjoy a visit. He's a bit tired and unsettled. A friendly face always helps."

Mandy and Gran smiled and said good afternoon to some of the patients who were reading or listening to the radio through earphones. At the end of the ward, Mandy spotted a man lying in a bed. He seemed to be asleep and looked pale and rather thin.

"That's Percy," Gran said.

As Mandy and Gran reached his bedside, Percy stirred and opened his eyes.

"Hello, Percy," Gran said gently. "How are you feeling?"

The old man looked up and raised his head. His faded blue eyes flickered over them.

"Where — where is he?" Percy muttered, his forehead creasing with worry. "Not . . . here . . ."

"Where's who, dear?" Gran said, leaning forward. "Who's not here?"

But Percy had sunk back onto the pillows. His lips moved, but he had closed his eyes again. His words came out in a whisper. "He's not here. . . . Where is he?"

"Oh, dear." Gran looked worried. "I think he must be asking about his son."

She turned to Mandy and explained quietly that Percy had lived with his son and his family. "But then his son received a very good job offer in America, so he's taken his family to live there for a year. Percy could have gone with them, but he wanted to stay in the family house in Welford."

"So Percy lives on his own now?" Mandy said, feeling concerned.

Gran nodded. "That's why I wanted to pop in and check on him. Come on, dear. I think Percy's gone back to sleep. We'll let him rest. It's the best thing for him. We can come back another time."

"OK," Mandy said. "I'll come with you next time." As she left Ward Twelve and went back toward the room where they were setting up, she couldn't help feeling worried about the confused elderly man.

Two

"That silver wrapping paper looks really good!" Mandy and Gran came back to find James and Grandpa hard at work.

"It's supposed to look like the walls of an ice cave," James explained. "At least, it will when it's finished."

"How is Percy?" Grandpa asked.

"He seemed a bit mixed up, didn't he, Gran?" Mandy said.

Gran nodded. "Poor fellow. I think he's still a bit shaken up by being sick."

"Gran and I are going to see him again tomorrow," Mandy said.

"Good idea," Grandpa agreed. "He might be feeling better by then."

James waved Mandy over to help him cover the next board. Mandy held the paper as James smoothed it down. They managed to cover half of another board before they ran out of paper.

"There's lots more in the van. I'll go get some," Mandy offered. She went down the hall and out the main doors. She was just going to walk across the parking lot when she stopped in her tracks.

A small brown-and-white Jack Russell terrier was standing a short distance away, watching her.

As soon as Mandy took a step toward it, the little dog backed away. Mandy stopped and crouched down. She knew that if she made herself look smaller, it would seem less threatening to the dog.

"Hello," she said gently. "What are you doing here, all on your own?"

The little dog whined softly. But although it wagged its long tail, it didn't come any nearer.

Mandy thought it seemed quite nervous. "I wonder who you belong to," she said softly. She looked around but could see no sign of an owner. The terrier looked well fed and was wearing a collar. Mandy didn't think it could be a stray.

She tried again, speaking in a coaxing voice and rubbing the tips of her fingers together encouragingly. "Come here. It's all right. I won't hurt you."

The little dog looked at her with intelligent brown eyes but stood its ground. Its ears twitched, and for a moment, Mandy's spirits lifted. It was going to come to her!

Suddenly, the dog gave another soft whine, then turned and dashed away into some shrubs.

Mandy felt a stab of disappointment. She stared after the dog, but it had disappeared into the shadows.

"Oh, it's that Jack Russell again," said a voice at her elbow.

Mandy turned to see the hospital aide who had helped them unload the van earlier. "Hello," she said. "So you've seen it here before? Do you know who it belongs to?"

The hospital aide shook his head. "It's been hanging around since yesterday. I've tried to catch it, and so have a couple of other people, but it won't let anyone near it. I'm not surprised that it's a little nervous, though. The poor thing was almost hit by an ambulance," he explained. "One of the guards told me he saw it run right in front of it. The dog had a lucky escape."

"Oh, no!" Mandy gasped. "No wonder it's scared." She felt worried about the Jack Russell. Someone must be missing it. And it had been around since yesterday. What was it eating? And where could it be sleeping?

"You seemed to know what you were doing just then," the aide said. "For a minute, I thought the dog was going to come to you."

Mandy smiled. "I love animals. My mom and dad are vets in Welford. I often help out in their clinic."

"Ah. That explains it," he said. "Well, I'd better go. I have a patient to take down to X ray."

"OK," Mandy said. "I'm going to have a quick look around the grounds. I might be able to find the dog."

"Good luck," the man said. "Let me know how you do."

"OK, I will. Thanks." Mandy smiled and set off toward the shrubs where the terrier had disappeared.

Ten minutes later, she had searched behind all the bushes on the narrow strip of lawn at the edge of the parking lot, and now she was looking underneath every parked car.

The light was fading fast, and it would soon be dark. There was no time to do a more complete search, so Mandy decided to head straight for the place outside the hospital cafeteria where the garbage cans were kept. If the dog was a stray, then maybe it would be hanging around there, looking for food. But again, she found nothing.

The Jack Russell was still on her mind when she went back to James and her grandparents.

"Don't you have it?" James glanced at her empty hands. "You've been gone for ages."

"Have what?" Mandy looked blank.

"The silver wrapping paper. Remember?" he said.

"Oh!" Mandy's hands flew to her mouth. "I completely forgot! Sorry."

"What have you been doing all this time?" Gran asked suspiciously.

Mandy gave an embarrassed grin. "There was a Jack Russell outside, all by itself. I tried to get close to it, but it ran off. The hospital aide said it had been here since yesterday. Maybe it's a stray, after all," she finished thoughtfully.

"Did you look for it?" James asked. He seemed to have forgotten all about wrapping paper now.

Mandy nodded. "I looked around the parking lot, but there was no sign of it."

Gran shook her head. "You and animals, Mandy Hope! And James is almost as bad!" She chuckled. "I expect that little dog's all tucked up in front of a cozy fire by now!"

Mandy remembered how well cared for the dog had looked and thought that her gran was probably right.

"Which dog?" said a familiar voice. It was Charlie again, his bright blue eyes wide with curiosity. "Is it yours, Mandy?"

"No," Mandy said. "I don't have any pets of my own. Dad says that we've got enough to do, looking after everyone else's animals!"

"Mandy's parents are both vets," James explained.

"Cool!" Charlie said. "So you get to share everyone else's pets!"

Mandy smiled at Charlie's eager face. "I suppose I do."

"Whose dog are you talking about?" Charlie wanted to know.

Mandy told him about the Jack Russell that had narrowly escaped being hit by an ambulance. "I searched for it, but it disappeared. I think it went back to its owner," she finished, sounding more sure than she felt.

Charlie's face lit up. "I love Jack Russells," he announced. "They're so lively!" But then he frowned. "I hope it *has* gone home. I've just been watching TV. The weatherman says it's going to snow tonight."

Mandy glanced across at James. She hated to think that there was a chance of the little dog spending the night outdoors.

"And talking about cozy fires," Grandpa prompted.

Gran took the hint. "Time to pack up and go home, I think."

"Oh. You said I could help you again!" Charlie protested. He seemed to be bursting with energy.

"You can," Mandy said. "You can help us clean up,

then we'll be back tomorrow to do the interesting part — decorating Santaland."

"OK." Charlie began throwing things back into boxes. "I'll come back then."

"Phew!" James whistled under his breath. "He's a real live wire, isn't he?"

But Mandy didn't hear him. She had a picture in her mind of a little brown-and-white dog with a sweet face. It was huddled in the shadows, shivering with cold, while thick snow fell all around.

"Bye, Mandy. Have a good Christmas!" Simon, the clinic nurse at Animal Ark, was crunching across the frosty gravel toward his car when Mandy arrived back home.

"Bye, Simon! You, too!" Mandy called. She waved as Simon drove out onto the road. He was going home to stay with his mom and dad.

Mandy went straight through the cottage and into the modern extension at the back, which housed her parents' clinic. The waiting room was crammed to bursting with sick pets. Their owners were eager to have the pets checked before the holidays. Through the open door of one of the examination rooms, Mandy glimpsed her dad lifting a pet carrier onto the table.

"If you'd like to take Tina in now." Jean Knox, the

gray-haired receptionist, sent in Dr. Emily's next patient, a kitten needing a routine injection.

Mandy took one look at the line of people waiting at the desk and asked Jean, "What needs to be done?"

"Oh, thanks, Mandy dear." Jean looked even more flustered than usual. She fumbled for her glasses, which usually hung on a chain around her neck.

"On top of your head," Mandy whispered.

"Of course. Thanks, dear." Jean pulled her glasses down to her nose. "Could you get this patient some worming pills, please? And this woman needs medicated shampoo for her poodle."

Mandy helped behind the desk for the next twenty minutes. She checked appointment details on the computer and handed out shampoo and worming pills to people who didn't need to see her mom or dad.

"Oh, good, you're back, Mandy!" Dr. Emily poked her head around the door of the second treatment room. "I need another pair of hands. Can you spare her, Jean?"

Jean said she could manage now, so Mandy went to help her mom. There was a huge gray rabbit on the treatment table. "Wow! It's enormous. What kind is it?" she asked, unhooking a white coat from behind the door and putting it on.

"A Flemish giant," her mom answered. "And they're

very strong. Hold him still, would you, dear?" Dr. Emily bent close as she cleaned the rabbit's cut foot. "How's Santaland coming along?"

"Fine." Mandy cradled the rabbit in both arms, holding it so that it didn't struggle. The rabbit's owner, a serious-faced boy of about ten, and his dad watched her.

"We had a boy named Charlie helping us," she told her mom.

Dr. Emily threw a used cotton pad into the trash and reached for a box of antibiotic powder. "So, do you think you'll finish it tomorrow? Your dad's eager to see his setting!"

"Mmm. I think so," Mandy murmured. The Jack Russell was still on her mind.

Her mom looked up and narrowed her eyes. "Out with it," she ordered kindly.

"Out with what?" Mandy blinked at her.

"Whatever's bothering you," Dr. Emily replied.

Mandy grinned. "Well, there was this sweet little dog at the hospital. I thought that he might be a stray." She repeated the saga of the Jack Russell. "So, what do you think?" she asked when she'd finished.

Her mom shrugged thoughtfully. "I'd say that your gran's probably right about the dog going home. But we'll talk about it later, when it's less busy, if you like. OK?"

"OK," Mandy agreed. "It's crazy out there. Everyone

in Welford seems to have brought their pet in for something!"

After the huge rabbit, Mandy helped her mom treat a cat with a gashed face and a Border collie with an eye infection. Then Jean needed more help in reception.

Clinic hours were almost over, and Mandy was back in the examination room getting ready to wipe down the examination table when the door opened. A stout woman in a tweed suit sailed in. It was Mrs. Ponsonby. Pandora, her pet Pekingese, was tucked under one arm, and Toby, her scruffy mongrel pup, trotted beside her on a leash.

"Oh, no. I wonder what's wrong this time?" Mandy whispered to her mom. Probably Mrs. Ponsonby's portly Pekingese had refused its tenth juicy treat or snuffled a bit too loudly. Pandora had to be the most spoiled pet in Welford!

"Hello, Mrs. Ponsonby," Dr. Emily said cheerfully, tucking a few strands of hair behind her ear. "What's the matter with Pandora?"

"Oh, Pandora's fine. Just darling, as usual!" Mrs. Ponsonby's bossy voice filled the room. "It's Toby I've come about."

"Oh." Dr. Emily raised her eyebrows at Mandy. "Let's get him up on the table, Mandy. What's the problem, Mrs. Ponsonby?"

"Well." The woman pursed her lips in annoyance. "I was outside the post office, mailing a Christmas card, when a rude young man came dashing out of the shop. He just pushed right past me! Toby gave a yelp, and I realized that the brute had trodden on his foot."

"Oh, poor you." Mandy petted the little mongrel's head. Toby yapped sharply and reached up to lick her chin. His tail was wagging wildly.

"I'd have given that young man what for!" Mrs. Ponsonby went on fiercely. "But he had already roared off in one of those flashy fast cars."

Lucky for him, Mandy thought. Mrs. Ponsonby would have made mincemeat out of him.

"Well, Toby doesn't seem too distressed," said Dr. Emily. "Which paw was it? I'll just check him over."

While Mandy soothed the wriggling dog, her mom ran expert fingers over his sore foot. Pandora looked on, untroubled, from Mrs. Ponsonby's arms. Her long creamy fur flowed over her owner's coat sleeve.

"There's some swelling, but it's not serious. I think the foot's just bruised," Dr. Emily said decidedly.

Toby wriggled and nudged Mandy's chin with his cold, wet nose.

"There's not much wrong with you, is there?" Mandy tickled his warm chest.

"I'd like to see him moving around. Could you put him on the floor, please, Mandy?" Dr. Emily asked.

Toby trotted around, sniffing the floor and poking into the corners of the room. Dr. Emily watched closely. At last she gave a satisfied nod. "He seems to be bearing his weight on that foot. I don't think we need to X-ray it."

"Oh, I'm so glad he's all right!" Mrs. Ponsonby bent over and scratched the top of her dog's rough little head. "Let's take you home, Toby dear, and find you a special treat."

Mandy rolled her eyes. If Toby wasn't careful, he was going to end up as portly as Pandora.

"Not too many treats," Dr. Emily advised.

Mrs. Ponsonby didn't seem to hear. "Thank you so much, Emily," she said cheerily, picking up Toby's leash and heading for the door. "I'll see you tomorrow, Mandy," she called over her shoulder. "I'm going to stop by to see how our Santaland has turned out."

"That's all we need." Mandy groaned as Mrs. Ponsonby closed the door behind her.

Dr. Emily chuckled and gave her daughter a hug. "Whatever you say about that woman, you have to admit that she loves those dogs!" She led the way into the reception room, where Jean was just putting on her coat.

"Bye, Jean. See you tomorrow." Mandy waved good-

bye and locked the clinic door behind her before join-
ing her parents in the kitchen.

"Supper!" Dr. Adam peeled off his white vet's coat
and hung it on the back of the kitchen door. "What I
wouldn't give for a poached egg on toast!" He groaned.

"Double allowance this week?" Mandy suggested
with a chuckle.

Dr. Adam made a face. "Nice try!"

Dr. Emily joined in the laughter. "You two make a
great act!" She went over to the sink to fill the kettle.
"Does everyone want tea?"

"I've just got to go and see Peaches first," Mandy said.
She went back through the clinic and into the residential unit where animals that were too sick to go home
were kept. Rows of wire cages filled the room, which
was spotlessly clean. Mandy went past each one, checking that the patients all had clean water and bedding.

Peaches was curled up on a pile of straw. Mandy
could see her shaved side and the neatly stitched inci-
sion. She put her face close to the cage and looked in.
Peaches's pink nose twitched, and she opened her gentle brown eyes.

"Oh, good. You're awake," Mandy said softly. "Aren't
you beautiful?"

Laura had told her that Peaches was an Abyssinian —
a rough-haired breed. The creamy coat grew in rosettes

all over Peaches's body, making her fur stand up in all directions.

Mandy put a finger inside the cage to pet the guinea pig. "I wonder if you're hungry." She went to the fridge and cut a small chunk of cucumber. Peaches could eat this safely as it wasn't leafy and cabbagey. Mandy opened the cage and put the morsel inside.

Peaches's pink nose twitched more rapidly. She leaned forward and butted the juicy treat but didn't touch it. Mandy noticed that she was still quite wobbly. She hoped that it was just the aftereffects of the anesthesia. "Now, you just get better, Peaches," she said in a soft voice. "And then Laura will come and take you home."

Peaches turned to look at her. She twitched her pink nose and gave a warbling chirrup. Then she turned her back on the cucumber and burrowed down into her clean straw.

"Have a good rest. I'll come and see you again tomorrow." Mandy was still worried about the guinea pig. Peaches seemed to be getting better, but she wouldn't regain her strength if she didn't eat something soon.

Three

Saturday morning dawned cold and crisp. Mandy looked out her bedroom window at the frost-covered grass. No sign of snow yet. She pulled on a warm sweater and her jeans, then dashed downstairs.

Dr. Adam was ironing his white vet's coat in the kitchen. He looked up and smiled. "You seem in a hurry!"

"I am!" Mandy said. "I'm meeting James. We're taking the bus over to Walton and meeting Gran and Grandpa at the hospital."

"Well, make time for breakfast," her dad said, wagging his finger jokingly. "It's the most important meal of the day."

"Yes, Dad!" Mandy rolled her eyes. Then she saw the pan on the stove. "Oh, great. Oatmeal!" She helped herself to a steaming bowlful.

Mandy blew on each spoonful as she ate it. A few minutes later, she jumped up from the table and rinsed the empty bowl in the sink. "Got to go!"

Dr. Adam was just slipping on his coat and getting ready for morning office hours. Mandy kissed his cheek. "See you later!"

As Mandy walked toward the Fox and Goose intersection, she saw James already waiting there. He had a duffel bag slung over one shoulder.

"Hurry up!" he shouted, waving frantically. "There's a bus coming."

Mandy sped up and arrived, out of breath, just as the bus pulled up. "We're going to be really early for meeting Gran and Grandpa," she said.

"Not if we stop by the pet shop," James said promptly, getting onto the bus.

"Why would we want to do that?" Mandy threw him a puzzled look as she paid her fare. "Apart from looking at all the animals."

"Which you'd just hate, of course!" James joked. "I

want to buy a Christmas stocking for Blackie. They have some really good ones."

"OK!" Mandy took a seat next to James as the bus drove through Welford village.

Twenty minutes later, they were opening the pet shop door. Mandy loved the rich smell of animal food and straw that greeted them as they went inside.

"Wow!" James looked wide-eyed at the display of Christmas gifts for animals. There were edible treats for every pet from parakeets and hamsters to cats and dogs. On one rack there were also toys — balls with bells inside, catnip mice, and plastic balls that dispensed treats while they were rolled.

"And look at these squeaky dog pull-toys and new leashes!" Mandy said.

"Yeah, they're great. But there are too many choices." James fiddled with his glasses and groaned. "I can't decide what to get."

"No contest." Mandy tilted her head. "A stocking, definitely! Otherwise, how will Blackie know it's Christmas?"

James laughed and reached for the biggest doggie stocking on the shelf. "Blackie's going to love this. He won't be able to move for a week once he's eaten all these treats," he said as he went to pay.

Mandy raised her eyebrows. Blackie keeping still and not demanding a walk? Not likely!

With the stocking safely stowed in James's bag, Mandy and James walked along the road to the hospital.

"Look, there's Gran and Grandpa's van," Mandy said, pointing across the parking lot.

As they approached the main door, a small brown-and-white dog came out from behind some bushes. It stopped when it saw them and hung back warily.

Mandy froze. "Look!" she whispered. "It's that Jack Russell again."

James stopped dead, too. He frowned. "Do you think it's been here all night?"

"It must be cold and hungry if it has," Mandy said worriedly. "I'm going to see if I can make friends with it."

She moved forward very slowly, careful to avoid direct eye contact with the little dog. "Hello again. Don't be afraid," she said soothingly.

The Jack Russell gave a soft whine and licked its lips nervously. It pattered sideways on its short legs but didn't run away. The metal tag on its collar jingled as it moved. Mandy peered at the tag, but she couldn't read what it said.

"I think it wants to be friends," James said in a low voice. "But it seems very timid."

The Jack Russell dipped its head, and it took a few steps forward. It whined softly.

Mandy held her breath. "That's it. Come here," she encouraged gently.

The dog blinked at her and moved closer still. Slowly, Mandy stretched out her hand and let the dog sniff it. A moment later, she felt a wet cold nose brush against her fingers.

"Good boy!" Mandy stroked the dog's white chest.

"Well done, Mandy," James whispered behind her.

"Isn't he handsome?" The Jack Russell had half closed his eyes, and Mandy risked stroking his soft ears. She was just reaching out her fingers to take hold of his collar when the little dog darted sideways and took off across the parking lot. "Oh, no." Mandy's spirits sank. Just when she was getting somewhere!

She turned around to look at James. Over his shoulder she saw a security guard coming toward them. He must have startled the dog.

The guard wore a broad grin. "You're the first person who's gotten anywhere near that crafty little beggar!"

"Crafty?" Mandy echoed, puzzled. "Why? What's he done?"

"Swiped a bag of chips earlier, that's what!"

"Were they yours?" James asked.

The guard shook his head. "A little girl dropped them as she was getting into a car. And that terrier popped out of the bushes, grabbed the bag, and took off. He's quite a character."

"Do you know who he belongs to?" Mandy asked.

"No. But I've seen him around here before." The guard shrugged and headed back to his station at the entrance of the lot.

"That's just what the aide said, isn't it?" James commented as they went in to meet Mandy's grandparents.

"Yes," Mandy agreed, feeling even more worried. "Do you think he's a stray?"

"Could be." James looked thoughtful. "We could ask around and see if any other people have seen him."

"Good idea," Mandy said. "At least we know he's had something to eat!"

"Yeah, chips," James said. "But that's not much for a hungry dog, is it?"

"No," Mandy agreed. Maybe they should start putting food down themselves, which would make it easier to get near the timid little dog.

"Hi!" Charlie said, looking up to greet Mandy and James the moment they walked into the room. He was sprawled on the floor in his plaid robe and bright yellow pajamas. Sheets of paper were spread out on the floor all around him. He was sticking glitter in the outlines of bold letters drawn on them. "It's going to be a banner.

For the front of the display!" Charlie explained, flashing them a wide grin.

Grandpa winked. "It was your gran's idea," he whispered to Mandy and James. "Charlie's spent all morning getting the lettering just right. He hasn't said he's bored once!"

"Good idea, Gran!" Mandy grinned. She told her grandparents about seeing the Jack Russell again. "Did you notice a little brown-and-white dog in the parking lot when you arrived?"

Gran shook her head. "No, dear. We didn't see any dogs, did we, Tom?"

Grandpa shook his head.

Charlie jumped up. "Is the dog outside again? Let's go and see him!"

"No. He's gone now," Mandy explained. "He came over to me, but the guard startled him, and he ran off again. We don't know where he is now."

"Oh," Charlie grumbled. "I really wanted to pet him."

"The guard said he stole a little girl's bag of chips," James told him.

Charlie laughed, forgetting his disappointment. "Did he?"

"Oh, dear. He could scare people, jumping up at them like that." Gran looked worried. "He didn't bite her, did he?"

Mandy quickly explained that the little girl had dropped her chips on the ground in the parking lot. "He's a really sweet little dog, Gran. I managed to pet him before he ran off."

"Maybe you'll see him again. We're going to be here until Christmas Eve. But don't get any ideas about taking home a stray dog," Gran warned.

"No way." Mandy sighed. "Not with Mom and Dad's rules."

For the next hour or so, she and James were very busy. They decorated the collection box for the donated presents. Then they began setting out the raffle prizes on a table.

"This table looks a little dull," James said, carefully balancing a large box of chocolates on its side.

"We could wind tinsel around its legs," Mandy suggested. "We've got tons of the stuff!"

"Good idea. I'll get some," James said.

"Mandy, where are the scissors?" Charlie's cheerful voice interrupted him.

When Mandy had passed him the scissors, Charlie decided he needed some tinsel to decorate the edges of his banner. Mandy was just helping him attach the tinsel with tape when a woman poked her head into the room. She was wearing jeans and a thick sweater. Her blond hair, round face, and blue eyes were similar to Charlie's.

She came straight over to them. "Hi! The nurse said you'd be in here. You two look very busy."

"Mom!" Charlie jumped up and gave her a hug. "Look what we're making!" He pointed to the banner.

"That's great," said the woman, ruffling Charlie's hair. She turned to Mandy. "Thanks for letting Charlie help. I know he can be a handful. He's got energy to spare."

"He's all right," Mandy said, smiling. She introduced herself and James. "And this is my gran and grandpa. We're decorating Santaland this year."

"I'm Linda Kingston," Charlie's mom said with a friendly smile. She took a box out of her shoulder bag and gave it to Charlie. "I thought you could use these." She beamed at Mandy and James. "My son's quite an artist."

"Colored pencils! And a new sketch pad! Thanks, Mom. These are great."

"What sort of things do you like to draw?" James asked.

Mrs. Kingston looked surprised. "Haven't you shown your new friends your pictures?" she asked her son.

Charlie looked down and shook his head, looking a bit embarrassed. He dug at the floor with the toe of his slipper.

"We'd love to see your pictures, wouldn't we, James?" Mandy said.

James nodded.

"Really?" Charlie's face lit up. "Come on, then. I'll show you. You come, too, Mom!"

They all trooped through to the children's ward. There was a huge Christmas tree in one corner, and decorations hung from the ceiling.

Charlie led them to his bed. Colorful drawings of animals were pinned up on the wall around it — lions, tigers, and elephants, but pictures of dogs outnumbered them all.

Mandy's eyes widened. "These are really good."

"Yeah!" James agreed. "Especially the ones of dogs."

Linda Kingston smiled proudly. "Drawing, painting, and dogs, that's all my Charlie's interested in. He's crazy about dogs. He's got a real way with them, too."

Charlie's blond eyebrows shot together in a fierce frown. "Too bad you won't let me have one, isn't it!" he burst out, stalking away.

Mandy watched Charlie stomping off down the ward in the direction of the bathrooms. His shoulders were hunched, and he had thrust his hands into his bathrobe pockets.

"Oh, dear." Charlie's mom sank onto the bed. "I shouldn't have said that."

"Would you like me to go after him?" James offered.

"Thanks, but it's probably best to let him calm down by himself," Linda Kingston said with a sigh.

"Why isn't Charlie allowed to have a dog?" Mandy asked curiously. "Don't you like them?"

"It's not that," Mrs. Kingston said. "I'd like a dog, too. But Charlie and I live in an apartment, and we don't have a yard for a dog to run around in. Besides, I have to work full-time, and you can't leave a dog on its own all day. It wouldn't be fair."

"No," Mandy agreed. She glanced at all the drawings of the dogs again. No wonder Charlie had been so interested in the frisky little Jack Russell in the parking lot.

He was probably hoping the dog was a stray that needed a home. *His* home!

"I'll wait here for Charlie if you want to get back to your grandparents," Mrs. Kingston said. "He'll cool off soon, and then he'll probably join you."

"OK. Tell him we'll see him later." Mandy and James retraced their steps back through the children's ward.

"Those dog drawings are fantastic, aren't they?" said James.

"They're wonderful," Mandy agreed. "It's a shame Charlie can't have a real dog, though."

James nodded. "I couldn't imagine life without Blackie!"

"But you wouldn't have him if you lived in an apartment with no yard, would you?"

"No way!" James admitted.

"I hate to say it, but I have to agree with Charlie's mom," Mandy said. But even though she couldn't argue with Mrs. Kingston's sensible attitude, she couldn't help feeling sorry for Charlie.

Four

"Just one last thumbtack. Ta-da!"

Mandy and James were standing on hospital chairs as they finished pinning Charlie's banner above the door to the finished setting.

Three nurses and some patients from the children's ward had stopped by for a look. They clapped and cheered as James and Mandy climbed down from their chairs. James reddened but performed a mock bow, which made everyone laugh.

"The Santaland is pretty splendid, even if I do say so myself!" Gran said.

"Top-notch," Grandpa agreed.

And it was. Silver display boards formed three sides of the ice cave. Two tall rectangular pillars framed the entrance, while small Christmas trees placed on either side of the door added a festive touch. Decorations glittered everywhere, and Charlie's banner wished everyone MERRY CHRISTMAS.

"Good idea of yours to cover those cardboard boxes to make pillars," Mandy said to James.

Grandpa chuckled. "And who would have thought we would use up that entire mountain of tinsel!" He looked at the raffle table, which Mandy and James had decorated. "Hmm. Hairy tinsel legs. Interesting!"

Mandy laughed. "We think it looks cool, don't we, James?"

James nodded.

"Time for a break," Gran announced when the nurses and children had gone back to the ward. "I packed some lunch. Egg salad sandwiches and cookies, anyone?"

"Great!" Mandy loved her gran's cooking, especially her cookies.

Gran was just gathering up the paper plates and napkins from their indoor picnic when the door opened and two young children and their mother looked in.

"We have our first visitors," announced Grandpa, ushering them in.

"We brought some things for the Christmas toy drive," the woman explained, while the children gazed round-eyed at the ice cave.

"How nice! Thanks very much," Gran said. "The box for them is over there."

"And don't forget to buy some raffle tickets!" Mandy reminded them. "It's for a good cause."

"And we've got some great prizes," James added.

All afternoon there was a steady stream of visits from local children and their parents. The toy drive on the radio seemed to be doing the trick.

"Good grief!" James peered into the collection box, which was filling up rapidly. "At this rate, we're going to need another box."

"Good. That means all the children in the hospital over Christmas will get lots of presents," Mandy said. Meanwhile, she took the opportunity to ask everyone she could about the Jack Russell. "Did you see a little brown-and-white dog on your way into the hospital?"

"No, sorry," came the reply from three children and their dad. It was the same story from the next two family groups. Then Mandy had some luck.

"Oh, yes! We just saw him!" said a little girl in a red hat.

Mandy's heart leaped. "Where?"

"Just going into the bushes at the side of the parking lot," her mom said. "Is he your dog?"

The bushes. Mandy's hopes rose. That was where she had seen him the first time. So the little dog was still around. Mandy shook her head. "We don't know who he belongs to. We think he's a stray."

"What a shame," the woman replied. "He looks very sweet."

He is, Mandy thought. She felt more and more worried about the Jack Russell. Snow was forecast for the next few days. She hated to think of the dog spending another night outside. There had to be something they could do. She couldn't get the thought of the Jack Russell's appealing face out of her mind.

"I'm going to visit Percy," Gran informed Mandy when the number of visitors bringing toys and raffle prizes had slowed a bit. "Do you want to come with me?"

Mandy jumped up at once and followed her gran along the hall to Ward Twelve.

"Oh, look!" Mandy saw that Percy was sitting up in bed. The old man was wearing glasses and reading a newspaper. "He must be feeling stronger."

"He's certainly a better color," Gran agreed as they approached the bed. "Hello, Percy. You're looking much better today," she said brightly.

Percy looked up and peered at them over the top of his glasses. He didn't smile. "Oh, it's you, Dorothy. Thanks for coming," he said politely.

"And I've brought my granddaughter, Mandy, to say hello," Gran said.

"Hi, Mr. Green," Mandy said, smiling.

"Nice of you to come," Percy murmured. But he kept staring down at the newspaper that lay on the bed, as if he was thinking about something else.

"Mandy's helping us with Santaland." Gran tried to engage Percy in conversation. "Her friend James is here, too, and Tom, my husband."

"And there's a boy named Charlie helping us. He's recovering from bronchitis," Mandy added.

"That's right." Gran smiled kindly at the old man. "Perhaps you might like to come and see us all later? It's just a short walk down the hall, past the children's ward."

"I'm sure it's very nice." Percy seemed to find talking an effort. "Thanks for coming to see me, Dorothy. But I'm rather tired. Would you mind . . ." He took off his glasses and lay back against his pillow.

Mandy glanced over at her gran. Percy had closed his eyes and obviously didn't want to chat.

"Well — we'll leave you to rest," Gran said. "We'll stop by again when you feel up to having visitors."

"Good-bye, Mr. Green," Mandy said quietly. She got no reply. It looked as if Percy might have fallen asleep.

"Oh, dear." Gran looked worried as she and Mandy

walked back to Santaland. "Percy seems so depressed, not at all like himself. He usually loves to chat. I think I'll have a word with Nurse Lacey."

They found the nurse in her office at the end of the ward. "Ah, yes," said Nurse Lacey in answer to Gran's inquiry. "Mr. Green. Physically he's almost back to normal. But he does seem very down. I can't quite understand what he's saying. Something about — a twinkle?"

"Twinkle?" Mandy said. "What on earth does he mean?"

"I think I can help you there," said a voice from behind them. "Twinkle is Dad's Jack Russell. I bought him to keep my father company while we were in America. I hope he's all right — I don't know what happened to him when Dad was brought into the hospital."

Mandy, Gran, and Nurse Lacey turned around. A tall man with dark hair who was wearing a blue suit stood there. He had a friendly face, but Mandy thought he looked tired.

"Hello, I'm Michael Green, Percy's son," he introduced himself. "I've driven straight here from the airport."

"I'm Dorothy Hope," Gran said. "I live in Welford, near Percy. And this is Mandy."

"Hello, Mr. Green," Mandy said.

"It's very kind of you to visit my father." Percy's son smiled at Gran and Mandy. "Please call me Michael."

Mandy smiled back. She liked Percy's son right away.

"Your father will be very pleased to see you," Nurse Lacey said to Michael. "He's much better. We've got the asthma under control now."

"Thank goodness for that. I was so worried," Michael said, then he grinned. "But by the sound of things, it's Twinkle he wants to see! Dad's always loved Jack Russells. He used to breed them in the old days."

"Did he?" Mandy was immediately interested.

"I had no idea," Gran said. "I used to see Percy when I took his meals-on-wheels. But I didn't know that he had a dog. Percy never invited me into the house, and I got the feeling he liked to keep to himself."

"That's Dad, all right," Michael said. "He's a proud man and likes to think that he can manage by himself. That's why I got him Twinkle. Dad might be shy with people, but I knew he wouldn't object to a dog keeping him company!"

Mandy smiled. "Dogs make wonderful friends, don't they?" she said. A picture of Charlie, who wanted a dog so badly, flashed into her mind.

Michael nodded. "Dad's still pretty famous in terrier racing, you know. He's bred some champion dogs."

"Really?" Mandy was fascinated by the idea that Percy had bred champion racers. Just wait until she told James — and Charlie!

"Oh, yes. Get him talking about terrier racing, and you can't get a word in edgewise." Michael turned to the ward nurse. "I think I'll go and see him now. If I can tell him about Twinkle, he's sure to feel much better."

Nurse Lacey nodded and smiled. Then she picked up a clipboard from the desk and bustled back out to her wards.

Michael turned back to Mandy and her gran. "By the way, who is looking after Twinkle while Dad's in the hospital?"

There was an awkward silence. Michael looked from Gran to Mandy. "Is Twinkle with Dad's next-door neighbor?" he prompted.

"I'm not sure." Gran looked worried. "I don't think anyone realized that Percy had a pet dog. As I said, *I* certainly didn't. Not until you just told me."

"What?" Michael frowned. "But Twinkle must have been with Dad when he was brought into the hospital. Didn't someone see him?"

"Oh." Mandy suddenly put two and two together. "I think I might have seen Twinkle," she burst out.

"Did you? Where?" Michael asked.

"In the parking lot," Mandy told him. "I've seen him a couple of times. An aide and a guard said that a Jack Russell has been hanging around outside the hospital for a couple of days. And some of the kids visiting our Santaland today saw him, too. It's got to be Twinkle."

"Slow down a minute, Mandy dear," Gran interrupted. "It could be a coincidence. Walton's quite a way from Welford. How would Twinkle have gotten here?"

Mandy frowned. Gran had a point. But she was sure that the stray was Twinkle.

"Didn't you say that you managed to get close to the dog this morning?" Gran said.

"Yes, that's right," Mandy answered.

"So you got a good look at him? Can you describe him?" Michael asked.

"He's almost all white," Mandy said, "with brown ears and a patch of brown over one eye. I managed to pet him, but he ran off. Then James and I spoke to the guard, and he told us about Twinkle stealing some chips."

Michael ran a hand through his dark hair. He looked worried. "It certainly sounds like our Twinkle. Especially the chips! He's a bit of a rascal. Can you show me where you last saw him? I should see if I can catch him."

"I'll help you," Mandy said. "If we go by Santaland, we can pick up James. He'll want to look for Twinkle, too."

"Those two are always on hand in any animal emergency," Gran said to Michael with a smile. "Animal crazy, both of them."

Michael glanced down at Mandy. "Well, if you and James can lead me to Twinkle, you'll be doing me a huge favor. I'm really worried about him being loose on the streets. And I hate to think how Dad's going to react if his best friend's missing."

"Oh, dear," Gran said. "That could really set poor Percy back."

"But when we find him, Percy will be happy, won't he?" Mandy pointed out.

"My granddaughter's such an optimist," Gran said. "I'll help you look as well. Tom won't mind keeping an eye on things here."

"OK. I'll meet you all in the parking lot in a few minutes," Michael said, beginning to walk away. "I'm going to go see how Dad is doing first. But I don't know what I'm going to say if he asks me about Twinkle."

Mandy hurried back along the hall to get James. They just had to find Twinkle, for Percy's sake.

But finding him was one thing; catching him would be another.

"What?" Mandy looked blankly at James. She had just finished telling him about Twinkle.

James was holding up his hands and waving them about. He shook his head and mouthed silently, no. No.

Suddenly, an eager voice rang out. "I'm coming to help look for Twinkle, too!"

"Uh-oh." Mandy made a face. She hadn't realized that Charlie was in the doorway behind her.

"I was trying to tell you that he was listening," James hissed.

"Now, Charlie." Grandpa took charge. "You know you have to stay inside the hospital. You can help me here."

Charlie's face fell. "I'm fed up with being in here," he grumbled. "I can't do anything."

"I know, boy," Grandpa sympathized. "It's not much fun being sick, is it? But I'm sure Mandy and James will tell you if they find Twinkle, won't you?"

"Of course we will," Mandy agreed warmly.

"Can I help you look after Twinkle when you find him?" Charlie asked Mandy.

"Hang on," said Grandpa. "We don't know that it definitely *is* Twinkle yet."

"I do!" Charlie said, a look of certainty on his face. "I can't wait to see him. He sounds great."

Mandy smiled. She felt just the same!

Just then, Gran poked her head around the door. "Ready, you two?" she asked. Mandy and James grabbed their jackets and followed Gran out to the parking lot. They stopped outside the door and looked around. There were lots of cars and people around — but no little brown-and-white dog.

"Here's Michael now," Gran said. "How's Percy feeling?" she asked as Michael came up to them.

"He was pleased to see me." Michael smiled. He was looking much more relaxed now. "Couldn't believe it was me at first. He thought I was still in the States."

"Did he ask about Twinkle?" Mandy asked.

Michael nodded. "I said I wasn't sure who was looking after him, which isn't exactly a lie, but I promised that I would go and find out. Is there any sign of Twinkle yet?"

"No," Gran answered, shaking her head.

"Oh, dear. I hope nothing's happened to him," Michael said. "Parking lots can be dangerous places for loose dogs."

"Maybe he's staying out of sight while it's so busy," James suggested.

"Yes," Mandy said. "Twinkle's had one near miss already with an ambulance. I don't think he'd go near any of the cars."

James nodded in agreement. "There's lots of places around here for him to hide." He waved his arm toward the thick bushes that ran along either side of the parking lot. Beyond the shrubs, a lawn stretched away to thick woodland on one side and a housing development on the other. If Twinkle had decided to venture out of the hospital grounds, it might be impossible to find him.

"OK. Where shall we start looking?" Gran went into action mode.

"Let's you and I work our way up and down the rows of parked cars," Michael suggested to Gran.

"And James and I will start over by those bushes," Mandy said. "Twinkle's been seen there a few times." She looked at James, who nodded, and they headed off.

"Maybe Twinkle's made himself a den." James's logical mind ran on ahead. "He might have found somewhere that's sheltered to sleep."

"Good thinking," Mandy said. "I'll check behind all the bushes and trees in these borders."

"And I'll check those sheds over there," said James, pointing to a group of wooden buildings that stood at the edge of the lawn, on the woodland side of the grounds.

Mandy spent a few minutes searching under bushes, then made her way around to the area where the garbage cans were kept. Even though she hadn't spotted the Jack Russell there before, it was the sort of place where a dog might go to look for food.

"Mandy! Over here." It was James's voice. Mandy hurried around the corner of the hospital toward the sound.

James was standing next to the wall. "Look at this!" he said.

Mandy saw that a huge silvery pipe led down from the hospital's upper floors. The base of it entered the wall about half a yard above the ground.

"What is it? It looks like a heating duct or something," she said. She could feel hot air blowing around her knees, where the pipe joined the wall.

"It is!" James said. "And look at this." He bent down and pulled an old cardboard box from underneath the bottom of the pipe. A crumpled chips bag was in the corner of the box, and a few white hairs were on the bottom, as if a hairy white body had been lying there recently. "I bet Twinkle's been sleeping in here."

"Oh, yes!" Mandy admired the little dog's cleverness.

James looked around him, frowning. "So — where is he now?"

Mandy shrugged. "He could be anywhere. I guess we keep on looking."

Suddenly, there was a yell. "Hey! Come back with those, you little squirt!"

Mandy and James looked at each other. "Isn't that —" Mandy began.

"Yes!" said James quickly. It was the voice of the security guard they had spoken to yesterday.

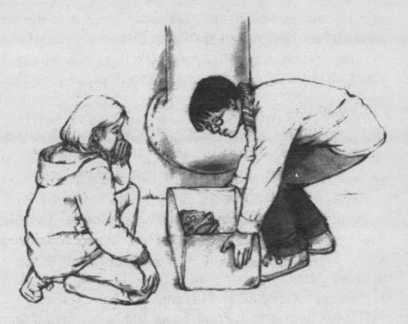

"Come on!" Mandy took off across the cement. She rounded a corner, with James hard on her heels. Racing across the lot, away from the guard's security cabin, was a small brown-and-white dog.

"Twinkle!" Mandy called out.

At the sound of his name, the dog turned. He gave a short bark and stood still.

"Is that his name?" the guard said. He went over to a squashed, plastic-wrapped package that lay on the ground and picked it up. "The little burglar stole my sandwiches," he grumbled. "I only turned my back for a minute, and he snuck in through the door and whipped them off the table! They're cheese and pickle, too. My favorite!"

Mandy's lips twitched. She saw that James was trying not to laugh. Then she grew serious. Twinkle was still standing just a few yards away. "This is the best chance we have of catching him," she whispered to James.

James nodded. "Let's try and get a bit closer to him."

Mandy and James moved forward slowly. Twinkle watched them closely. Every time they moved, he backed away. The little dog whined, his tail hanging between his legs. Mandy's heart sank. He seemed so wary. His brown ears were flat, and his muscles were tense.

"I think he wants to come to us, but he's worried that he's going to get in trouble for stealing those sandwiches," James reasoned.

"You could be right." Mandy saw that Twinkle was darting back and forth on his tiny paws, looking uncertain whether to take off again. "Poor little thing. He must be so cold and hungry," she said. Just then, a car door slammed. Twinkle froze, his ears straining toward the sound, and then he raced off behind the security cabin and disappeared into the bushes again. Mandy thought of Percy lying in his bed, worrying about Twinkle. He was going to be so upset when he knew that his dog was running around loose! They needed something to coax Twinkle into coming closer. But what?

"James!" she burst out suddenly. "I've just had a great idea!"

Five

James listened carefully while Mandy outlined her plan.

"Good idea!" he said. "I'll go get it right now. It's still in my duffel bag." He zoomed away and disappeared through the main entrance of the hospital.

"Get what?" Gran had just arrived at the security cabin, with Michael beside her. "I know that look, Mandy Hope. What are you and James plotting?"

"We need something to persuade Twinkle to come to us, right?" Mandy began.

"Right," Gran agreed. "What are you going to use?"

"Well — Twinkle must be starving," Mandy said. "He just tried to sneak off with the guard's sandwiches."

"Is he nearby?" Michael looked around hopefully.

Mandy shook her head. "He was, but he ran away when someone made a noise. I don't think he went far, though. James and I thought we could use food to tempt Twinkle nearer when he comes back."

"Good thinking, Mandy." Michael smiled at her. "Tell you what, why don't I give Twinkle a call to see if he appears?"

"OK," said Mandy. "He might recognize your voice. Try over there first." She pointed to the bushes behind the security cabin.

Michael walked over and put his hands up to his mouth. "Twinkle!" he called. "Twinkle! Come here, boy!"

There was a rustle under one of the bushes, and a white nose peeped out. Mandy crouched down and peered into the leaves. Two big brown eyes blinked nervously in the gloom. Mandy held out her hand. "It's all right, boy," she said in a soft, calm voice. "No one's going to hurt you."

Twinkle took a cautious step forward. Mandy didn't move a muscle. Twinkle gave a little whine and walked out a few more inches. He looked around him, still tense and ready to run away.

"Well done, Mandy," Michael said quietly.

Just then, James burst out of the hospital doors and came running back across to them. He arrived red-faced and out of breath. "Oh, good. Twinkle's here!" James gasped. He came to a halt a few yards away. Twinkle watched him, but he didn't run away. James unzipped his coat and pulled out a long object covered in red-and-green cellophane. He held it up. It was Blackie's Christmas stocking.

"Thanks, James." Mandy didn't waste any time. She stood up and went over to James. Ripping open the cellophane, she took out a bag of doggy treats. She glanced across to the narrow strip of lawn beside the bushes where Twinkle was now standing. His ears were down, and he kept licking his lips nervously. *Just hang on a little longer, Twinkle*, Mandy pleaded silently.

"Where did that stocking come from?" Michael said to James.

"I bought it this morning at the pet shop. Think of it as a present to Twinkle — from my dog, Blackie!" James replied with a grin.

Gran turned to Mandy. "I wonder whether Michael should try to catch Twinkle. He did come back when Michael called him, didn't he?"

Michael shook his head. "Actually, Twinkle's not that used to me. He spent all his time with Dad, and I've been out of the country for months. I think you should try, Mandy. Twinkle came to you earlier. And he listened to you again just now."

"OK." Mandy didn't waste time arguing. She moved forward slowly. She hoped Twinkle would remember her. He had let her scratch his chest and pet his ears earlier that morning. Maybe he would trust her enough to take some of the dog treats. "Here, boy," she called. She put a few treats on the palm of her hand and held them out temptingly. "Come and see what I've got for you."

At first, Twinkle backed away. Then he lifted his nose and took a long, deep sniff. His ears shot upright, and he began to wag his tail.

He can smell the treats, Mandy thought. She took a few more steps toward him. "That's it. Come on. These are for you." She rustled the bag encouragingly. Twinkle's ears twitched at the tempting sound. Mandy's whole body was tense. Would her plan work?

Just then, a car pulled up behind her, looking for a parking space. Twinkle shied away and darted sideways, peering over his shoulder nervously.

"Oh, no!" Mandy remembered the ambulance. She was afraid that Twinkle would take off again, even though he was hungry. Then they would have to start all over again.

"Now what do we do?" Michael sounded as if he was out of ideas.

Suddenly, Mandy remembered one of Blackie's dog training classes. "When you call a dog toward you, you have to be really enthusiastic," the instructor had said. "The dog has to think he's missing out on something wonderful."

Mandy poured a few more treats into her hand. "Mmm. These taste so good!" she said in a high-pitched, excited voice. She pretended to be eating them, smacking her lips. "Yummy!" Out of the corner of her eye, she watched Twinkle, who was crouched under one of the bushes.

Twinkle put his head to one side. He seemed to be listening to Mandy as she appeared to eat the treats. Then he gave a little yelp of excitement and trotted toward her.

Mandy beamed as Twinkle pushed his cold nose into her hand. "Oh, good boy!" she praised him.

Twinkle crunched up all the dog treats. Then he gave a sharp bark. *More, please*, he seemed to be saying.

"You must be starving, you poor boy!" Mandy fed Twinkle more of the treats as James, Michael, and Gran walked cautiously toward them.

"You ought to be an actress," Michael said. "You nearly had me trotting over to sample those dog treats!"

Twinkle didn't look up when the others approached. He just kept eating, his long tail wagging frantically.

"Look at that! He's almost scarfed the whole stocking," James said, crouching down and petting Twinkle's ears. "I'll have to go get another one for Blackie."

"Oh, sorry, James." Mandy felt a bit guilty. "I hadn't realized how hungry Twinkle was!"

"It doesn't matter. I'm glad we were able to catch him," James said.

Suddenly, Twinkle stopped eating. Mandy slowly stretched out her fingers and took hold of his collar in case he decided to run away again. But the little dog didn't seem to want to go anywhere. He gave a friendly whine, then reached up and began licking James's chin.

"He's saying thanks for the treats," Mandy said, laughing.

"I think you're right!" Michael patted James on the shoulder. "That was a great idea!"

"Maybe someone should go and tell Percy that Twinkle's all right," Mandy suggested.

"You read my mind," Michael said. "He'll be so pleased to know that Twinkle is OK."

"I told you they were expert animal rescuers!" Gran patted her hair. A few gray strands had escaped from her bun.

"Mandy, could you bring Twinkle over to my car?" Michael asked. "I don't want him running away again while I go see Dad."

Mandy carefully picked up the little dog and held him in her arms. Twinkle gave a contented yap, and his mouth lolled open in a doggy grin.

Gran laughed. "Wouldn't it be nice if Percy could actually see that Twinkle's all right?" she said, reaching out and smoothing Twinkle's white coat. The dog was surprisingly clean, considering that he had been living outdoors for a couple of days.

Michael nodded. "But he's going to have to wait until he gets home for that."

"Maybe not!" Mandy said. Gran had given her an idea.

"What do you mean?" James asked.

"Well, Ward Twelve is on the ground floor, isn't it?" Mandy answered, warming to her idea. "And Percy's bed is next to a window. If someone holds Twinkle up, Percy could see him."

"That's a great idea!" said James. He began figuring out where Percy's room was. "The children's ward is in that wing." He pointed across the parking lot. "So Santaland must be there, and Ward Twelve is just around the corner, over there."

Still holding Twinkle, Mandy led the way past the hospital entrance and around the corner. A long, paved area ran the length of the wing, underneath the windows. Comfortable-looking wooden benches on which patients could sit and enjoy the sunshine in warmer weather stood along the wall.

Michael grinned. "I'll go over there and hold Twinkle up to the window right now. Dad's going to be delighted to see him safe and sound!" He lifted Twinkle out of Mandy's arms. Twinkle tensed briefly but then relaxed as Mandy slipped him another treat.

"We'll go and tell your dad to look out the window," Mandy volunteered.

"Good idea," said Michael. "I'll be waiting."

"What still puzzles me," Gran said as she, Mandy, and James made their way through the hospital to Ward Twelve, "is how Twinkle managed to follow Percy all the way to the hospital."

"It's a mystery, isn't it?" Mandy said.

"Maybe Percy knows something about it," James suggested.

They found Percy sitting up in bed, propped against his pillows. He was listening to the radio and looking rather glum.

"Hello again." Gran gave Percy a huge smile. "We've brought you some wonderful news."

"Oh," Percy said dully. He looked up at them briefly, then down at the bedcovers again.

"It's about Twinkle," James announced.

"Eh?" Percy sat up straighter. His whole face brightened. "Twinkle! You've seen him?"

"Oh, yes," Mandy said. "He's great!"

"And Michael's going to hold — *ow*!" James grimaced as Mandy stepped on his foot.

"Don't give it away!" she hissed out of the corner of her mouth.

"Sorry." James hopped around on one foot.

Percy didn't notice. He was craning his neck to peer down the hall behind them. "Where's Michael? Has he found out who's looking after Twinkle?"

"He certainly has." Gran pointed out the window. "Take a look."

Mandy saw Michael's face appear at the ground-floor window. He waved at his dad. Then he lifted Twinkle up so that the little dog could see into the ward.

Percy's eyes opened wide. He looked amazed. "Twinkle! You're here. I can't believe it!"

Twinkle had seen Percy, too. He let out a series of high-pitched yaps and wriggled in Michael's arms. His brown ears flapped wildly as he tried to get to his owner.

A huge grin spread across the old man's face. He waved back. "Well, I never. Well, I never. My little Twinkle's come to see me."

Michael signaled that he was going to come in and see his dad. He lowered Twinkle again and disappeared.

Percy sank back against his pillows, a contented smile on his face. "Oh, it's good to see that little rascal again," he murmured happily.

"We've been wondering how Twinkle got here. He's

been hanging around the hospital grounds for the past couple of days," Gran said.

"Is that where he was?" Percy shook his head slowly. "I should have known that he'd follow me here."

"But how did he get here?" Mandy asked. "What happened to Twinkle when you became ill?"

Percy looked thoughtful. He took a sip of water and made himself more comfortable on his pillows. "Well, young lady. Twinkle's a bit of an escapologist, and I'd got a piece of loose fence in my yard. I didn't want him getting out and running away, so I was in the yard checking out that fence. Then my asthma came on, and I don't really know what happened after that. . . ." He trailed off, looking worried.

Mandy's gran reached over and patted his hand. "Don't worry, Percy," she said. "Your neighbors saw you fall over, and they called the ambulance."

Percy nodded. "That's right. That's what the nurse told me."

"Was Twinkle with you in the yard?" Mandy asked. She still couldn't figure out how Twinkle had known where his owner had gone.

"Yes, he was playing with a ball down at the end of the yard," Percy said.

"So Twinkle must have gotten out of the yard and followed the ambulance," James guessed. "Maybe through the hole in the fence?"

"But how did he keep up with the ambulance?" Gran asked.

Mandy wondered about that, too. Jack Russells were strong little dogs, but Walton was twenty minutes by car from Welford.

Percy's face creased in a grin. "I figure he must have followed the ambulance all the way here. Probably took a few shortcuts across the moors to keep up."

"Wow!" James and Mandy looked at each other in astonishment. Mandy realized that Twinkle must be extremely devoted to his owner.

"Twinkle's as smart as they come," Percy said. He looked very proud of his enterprising pet. His pale blue eyes were shining, and there was a bit of color in his thin cheeks. "He'd have been a fantastic racer," Percy went on. "Racers have to be smart as well as fast to be winners, you know."

"Just wait until we tell Charlie all this!" Mandy said to James.

"Charlie? Is that the boy you mentioned earlier?" Percy said. "The one who's had chest problems, like me?"

"That's right. He's had bronchitis," Mandy told him. "He's pretty bored now that he's feeling better, and he's been helping out at Santaland, hasn't he, Mandy?" James added.

Mandy nodded. "And Charlie's dog crazy. He wanted to help us look for Twinkle, but he's not allowed outside the hospital yet."

"Bored, is he, eh?" Percy looked amused. "You tell him to come and see me. If he loves dogs, he might like to hear about my terrier racing days."

"I'm sure he'd love that!" said Mandy. She exchanged a grin with James.

Just then, Michael came striding into the ward. His dark blue suit was speckled with white dog hairs, but he didn't seem to mind. "Hello again, Dad!" He came straight over and gave Percy a hug. "It's good to see you looking more cheerful."

Percy patted his son's back. "I'm feeling much better, son. Especially now that I know Twinkle's OK! Where have you left him?"

Michael pulled up a chair next to Mandy's gran and sat down. "In the car I rented at the airport. He'll be fine for an hour or so. I've made a snug bed for him out of a travel rug and left a window open a tiny bit."

"Inside your car?" Percy looked a bit concerned.

Michael chuckled. "I know Twinkle's clever, but even he can't get out of a locked car! Don't worry. He'll stay put this time."

"It's not that," Percy said. "If Twinkle tries to escape he could do some damage to the seats and whatnot. He's small, but he's got sharp claws!"

"Oh, I see." Michael looked none too pleased at the thought of shredded seats in his rented car. "I don't know where else he'd be safe for an hour or so. I guess I'll just have to hope he behaves himself."

Mandy had an idea. "I've thought of somewhere. Hang on. I'll be back!" She turned to James. "Come on!" she said, jumping out of her chair and heading down the ward.

James hurried after her. "Where are we going?"

Mandy glanced back over her shoulder. "To have a word with Nurse Lacey!"

Six

"And if Twinkle is allowed into Santaland, Percy will feel better because he knows that his dog isn't cooped up in a car. And the people who come to bring presents will enjoy seeing Twinkle." Mandy stood in the ward nurse's office and explained her bright idea.

"Hmm. We really can't have a dog running around near the wards." Nurse Lacey looked doubtful.

"Oh, he wouldn't run around," Mandy assured her quickly. "Twinkle's really well behaved. We'd keep a close eye on him, wouldn't we, James?"

James nodded. Just then, the phone rang. The ward

nurse smiled at them and answered it. "Yes? This is Nurse Lacey speaking."

"Twinkle well behaved!" James whispered, raising his eyebrows at Mandy. "Have you forgotten about him stealing those sandwiches?"

"No." Mandy looked determined. "But I call that showing initiative! Twinkle will be fine now that he's had something to eat and seen Percy again, of course."

"I hope so!" James said quietly. He sounded less confident than Mandy.

"OK. Bye." The nurse put down the phone and turned back to Mandy and James. "Sorry about that. All right. I've decided that you can bring Twinkle inside. But you must be responsible for him."

"Great! Thanks very much!" Mandy said delightedly.

"Let's go and tell Percy and Michael," James said.

They hurried back to Ward Twelve. Mandy blurted out the good news the minute she reached Percy's bedside. "We have permission to bring Twinkle into the hospital — he's going to be allowed into Santaland!"

"Well, I never," Percy said. His blue eyes twinkled at her. "How did you manage that?"

"Mandy can be very determined where animals are concerned!" Gran told him, passing the end of his bed with a tray of pitchers. She had busied herself filling water pitchers and tidying up the vases of flowers while Percy spent some time with his son.

Mandy grinned. "Well, they can't speak up for themselves, can they?"

"There you are, Dad. You can be sure Twinkle will be in good hands." Michael seemed delighted by Mandy and James's news, too.

"Yes." Percy looked relaxed and happy now. "And will young Charlie be there, too?" he asked.

Mandy nodded. "Probably. Especially if he knows there's a dog around."

Percy chuckled. "Don't forget to tell Charlie to come and visit me. I guess we've got a few things in common."

Gran looked at Mandy with a slight frown. "Speaking of Charlie," she said, "you ought to go back and rescue your grandpa. That boy might have worn him out by now!"

Mandy grinned. "Don't worry, Gran. I'm sure Grandpa's kept him busy. Anyway, he was only worried about Twinkle."

"Better go tell Charlie you found him," Percy said to Mandy and James. "We don't want the boy to be worrying."

"I'll stay with Dad, if that's all right with you. We have a lot of news to catch up on." Michael stood up and took the belt off his raincoat. "Here you are. You can use this as a leash for Twinkle."

"Good idea. Thanks." Mandy pocketed the belt. She looked at James. "Do we have any of those dog treats left?"

James felt in one of his pockets and fished out a crumpled bag of treats. "Yup," he said, waving them at Mandy. "Although I can't believe that Twinkle could still be hungry."

Michael handed them his car keys. "No need to bring them back. I'll get them when I pick Twinkle up."

"OK," Mandy said. She waved good-bye to her gran, who was almost hidden by an enormous bunch of flowers belonging to a man at the end of the ward. Then she and James headed back to the parking lot.

"Now . . . which one is Michael's car?" James scanned the parking lot.

"Maybe that one?" Mandy said innocently. "The one with the Jack Russell looking out of the side window?" She went over to the sleek silver car and unlocked the door. Twinkle scrabbled through the seats and greeted her with an enthusiastic lick.

"Come on, boy," said Mandy as she slipped Michael's belt through his collar. As soon as the makeshift leash was on, Twinkle settled down and hopped obediently out of the car. After locking the car again, Mandy and James walked back across the parking lot and into the hospital, with Twinkle trotting calmly beside them.

"Cool!" Charlie's eyes nearly popped out of his head as Mandy led Twinkle into Santaland. "Mr. Hope! Look who's here!"

Grandpa had been adding more raffle prizes to the display on the table. He came over and gave Mandy a hug. "So your stray *was* Twinkle after all? Good for you!" He bent down and ruffled Twinkle's ears. The little dog responded with a friendly lick.

Just then Gran came back into the room. "I left Percy chatting with his son. He really seems to have perked up in the last hour." She glanced at the piled-up prizes and overflowing bin of donated presents. "My word, you've been busy, Tom!"

"Good thing I had some help, wasn't it, Charlie?" Grandpa said.

But Charlie didn't answer. He was already on his knees, making friends with Twinkle. "How come you brought Twinkle in here? Is he hungry? Can I pet him?" Charlie's questions tumbled over each other.

As Mandy and James explained how they had finally caught Twinkle, the terrier stood patiently at their feet, looking up at them with his mouth open, as if he was smiling. He seemed to know that everyone was talking about him.

"He certainly seems like a friendly little dog," Grandpa remarked.

"Of course he is!" Charlie said at once. "Jack Russells are great dogs. Twinkle's just the best!" He held up one finger and said firmly, "Sit, Twinkle."

Twinkle promptly sat down. His tail thumped against the floor as he looked up at Charlie expectantly.

"Good boy," Charlie said. "It's much nicer in here than in that parking lot, isn't it?"

Twinkle cocked his head and gave a gruff little bark.

"Look at Twinkle. He's listening to Charlie's every word," Mandy whispered to James.

James answered in a low voice. "I guess they're two of a kind. Both full of mischief!"

Mandy chuckled. James was right!

"I'm going to ask the nurse for a bowl," Charlie decided. "Twinkle wants a drink." He dashed out into the ward. A couple of minutes later he returned, carrying a plastic bowl filled with water. "There you are." Charlie put the bowl on the floor.

Twinkle began lapping up the water with his small pink tongue. Charlie watched with a grin on his face. "Look at that! He was really thirsty."

"I'm not surprised, after all those dog treats!" Gran

commented. "Now, it's all very well to make sure that Twinkle is fed and watered, but what about us? I'm famished!"

Mandy glanced at her watch and noticed with surprise that it was long past lunchtime.

James nodded eagerly. "I'm starving, too," he said.

Gran laughed. "It's a good thing I brought us some lunch, then, isn't it? Give me a hand with this, please, James."

James darted forward and helped Mandy's gran heave a basket onto an empty table. He delved into it and started handing out sandwiches.

They were just finishing their lunch when a new batch of people arrived with more wrapped toys for the Christmas toy drive. Gran, Grandpa, Mandy, and James soon had their hands full, seeing to the visitors. James helped stack the presents in front of the display boards when the collection box was full. Mandy was in charge of the raffle table. The tickets were selling like hotcakes.

"Would you like me to look after Twinkle?" Charlie offered eagerly. He had been back up to his ward for some lunch and a checkup, but he soon reappeared, making straight for Twinkle, who was sitting under the raffle table. Mandy had fastened one end of the makeshift leash to a table leg to prevent the dog from getting away again.

"You'll have to be careful that he doesn't run around," Mandy said. "We don't want him to trip the visitors."

Charlie looked serious. "OK. I'll just play with Twinkle quietly," he promised. He untied the belt and began to lead Twinkle around the back of the display. "I know! I'm going to make him something."

"What are you going to make him?" James asked as Charlie squeezed past him.

Charlie lifted his chin. "It's a secret!" he said importantly, disappearing behind the display boards.

"Don't worry," said Mandy. "He can't get into much mischief back there. There's only a few pieces of cardboard and some leftover decorations."

"Mandy! James!" Gran called to them. It was getting hectic again in Santaland, and their help was needed.

Fifteen minutes later, Charlie came out from behind the screen. He looked very pleased with himself. "Stay. That's a good boy," Charlie said to Twinkle, who was still out of sight. "Everyone, get ready!"

Mandy and James looked around. Gran, Grandpa, and the people visiting Santaland all stopped what they were doing. Charlie had everyone's full attention.

Mandy wondered what Charlie had been up to with Twinkle. There hadn't been a sound from either of them, apart from an occasional rustling and a muffled giggle from Charlie.

"Come on out, Twinkle!" Charlie called.

Twinkle trotted into view. Fixed to his head by bright red ribbons were two small antlers! They were made from cardboard and were rather wobbly, which gave him a lopsided appearance. Twinkle didn't seem to mind wearing them at all. His whole body wriggled, and his tail wagged furiously as he padded into the middle of the room.

Mandy and James burst out laughing. "With that headgear I guess he can be Dad's — I mean Santa's — honorary reindeer," said Mandy.

There was a ripple of applause from the visitors. A sturdy toddler dashed forward, arms extended, ready to make a grab for Twinkle.

Mandy tensed. She knew that dogs sometimes found small children unsettling.

She was about to move forward when Charlie sprang into action. "Sit, Twinkle," he said calmly.

Twinkle gave a short bark. Then he sat down with his nose in the air. The toddler threw his arms around Twinkle's neck and squeezed tight. Twinkle didn't blink an eye. The friendly little dog seemed to be taking all the fuss in his stride.

"Nice doggie!" The toddler petted Twinkle's back with a pudgy hand.

"Well done." Gran patted Charlie's shoulder. "You handled that well."

"I'm going to make sure Twinkle behaves himself," Charlie said seriously. "Lie down, Twinkle."

Twinkle promptly sank down. He lay on the floor and put his head between his front paws. His brown-and-white eyebrows moved up and down as he watched Charlie closely.

"Good boy." Charlie patted Twinkle's head.

"Look at that!" Mandy was very impressed. "Twinkle's being as good as gold!"

"Charlie's really great with him, isn't he?" James said.

"He's a natural!" Mandy agreed. "What a shame he can't have a dog of his own."

An hour later, Michael came by to get Twinkle. Mandy and James went over to have a word with him.

"How's your dad feeling?" Mandy asked.

"Much better, thanks," Michael told them. "In fact, he's so much stronger that Nurse Lacey says he'll probably be allowed out of bed tomorrow."

"That's great news!" Mandy said.

Tomorrow was Sunday, the day before Christmas Eve. It looked as if Percy might be well enough to go home for Christmas.

Twinkle was in the center of an admiring group of grown-ups and children. He sat with his head in the air, his tail thudding on the floor, as two small children petted him.

"What's Twinkle got on his head?" Michael caught a glimpse of Twinkle as the children moved away. "Oh, my goodness — antlers!" A huge smile spread across Michael's face.

"It was Charlie's idea to make them," Mandy explained, pointing to Charlie, who was standing on the other side of the display, examining one of the presents.

Michael seemed to be trying not to laugh. "They're very realistic. And Twinkle certainly seems to like them."

Charlie looked over at them. "Hi, I'm Charlie," he said to Michael. "Twinkle is going to be a pretend reindeer for Santa."

"Hello, Charlie." Michael grinned down at the boy. "That sounds like a great idea."

Charlie nodded and bent down to straighten one of the antlers, which had flopped forward. "I don't think Twinkle minds, you know," he said seriously. "I wouldn't have made him wear the antlers if he didn't want to."

"I'd better take Twinkle home with me now," Michael said. He smiled at Mandy's gran. "I'm staying at Dad's house over Christmas, so the nurses can get in touch with me if they need to."

Charlie carefully untied Twinkle's antlers. "I'll keep these safe for when he wants them again," he said.

"You do that," said Michael. "In fact, Charlie, I was going to ask you a favor."

"Oh?" Charlie glanced up at the tall man, looking puzzled.

"Yes," Michael continued. "If you have time, would you mind going to Ward Twelve to visit my dad? He misses Twinkle, and it might cheer him up if you told him about the antlers."

Charlie's face brightened. "OK. No problem! I'd like to meet him."

Mandy turned to Charlie. "Oh, I almost forgot to tell you. Percy, Michael's dad, used to breed racing terriers."

"Did he? Cool!" Charlie said. "I'd like to breed dogs when I grow up." He looked down at Twinkle again and ran his hand along the smooth white coat.

Michael took hold of Twinkle's makeshift leash. "I have to go now. I brought some work with me, and I'd better get started on it. See you all tomorrow."

"Bye." James and Charlie waved as Michael went out of the room. Twinkle trotted beside him, his claws clicking against the floor.

Mandy waved, too, but something had begun to bother her.

James took one look at Mandy's face. "What's wrong?" he asked.

"I was just thinking," she said worriedly. "If Michael's got so much work to do, who's going to take Twinkle for walks?"

Seven

Mandy poured herself a bowl of cereal and ate it while she looked out the kitchen window, admiring the frosty, bare branches of the trees in the yard. It was Sunday morning. There were only two more days before Christmas, and there was lots to do in the clinic. The hospital Santaland, however, *was* ready for Santa's visits.

Twinkle was on her mind as she finished her cereal. She wondered if Michael had found time to take him for a morning walk. She rinsed the bowl in the sink and went into the residential unit.

"Hello, dear." Dr. Emily was already there, studying one of the clipboards that held a patient's notes.

"Have you looked at Peaches yet?" Mandy asked.

"No." Dr. Emily shook her head. "But I've checked the kitten with the swollen leg, the poodle with the eye infection, and the rat with a stomach tumor. I left Peaches until last. I thought you might like to check on her."

"Thanks, Mom." Mandy looked into Peaches's cage.

The guinea pig was snuffling around in her straw. She gave a throaty little grunt and came over to the bars of the cage.

"How are you today?" Mandy poked her finger inside and tickled Peaches's nose. She could see the bare shaved patch on the guinea pig's side. The wound looked clean. "No signs of inflammation," she reported to her mom. "Peaches's eyes look bright, and her nose is nice and clean."

Dr. Emily came over to look, too. "She seems pretty alert this morning," she observed.

"She's doing really well!" Mandy was thrilled by Peaches's progress. "May I give her a treat?"

Her mom nodded. "There's lots of fresh vegetables to choose from. But no brassicas, remember."

"OK." Mandy knew that guinea pigs loved celery. She cut a piece, then opened the cage and put it inside. Peaches's pink nose twitched. She came forward and butted the celery. Her little round-tipped tongue poked out, and she took a tiny taste.

"Look!" Mandy said excitedly. "She's interested in it. That's a good sign, isn't it?"

"It certainly is!" Dr. Emily nodded. "I think there's a good chance that Peaches will be going home for Christmas. I know Laura will be pleased. When I spoke to her on the phone this morning, her mom said she had really missed Peaches."

As Mandy changed the guinea pig's bedding and checked her water bottle, she began to think about Twinkle again. She wondered if Twinkle still missed Percy. The little dog wouldn't want to stay at home if Michael had no time to give him some attention. "Got it!" she burst out. "Got to go, Mom! See you later."

"Off on a mission?" her mom asked, giving her a shrewd look.

"Yes. Operation Twinkle! And James is going to help. But he doesn't know it yet!" Mandy replied, dashing to the phone.

James answered on the third ring. "Hello?"

"Hi, James. Can you meet me at Gran's?" Mandy came straight to the point. "I've just had a great idea."

"Uh-oh! Another one!" James joked, but he sounded interested. "Fine. I'll be there as soon as I've had breakfast."

"Great. And bring Blackie with you!" Mandy put down the phone and dashed upstairs to put on a thick sweater and warm boots.

*   *   *

"Hello, Mandy dear. I saw you from the window." Gran opened the door to Lilac Cottage as Mandy reached the path. She looked up at the yellow-white sky. "If you ask me, that sky is full of snow," she warned.

"I hope so!" Mandy said. "I love white Christmases. Oh, good. Here's James."

"Hi, Mandy. Hi, Mrs. Hope." James struggled to stop Blackie from jumping up as he opened the gate and walked carefully down the frosty path.

"Hello, Blackie!" Mandy bent down to pet the Labrador's velvety ears. Blackie pushed his cold, wet nose into Mandy's hand. He wriggled vigorously, inviting her to play with him.

Gran laughed. "Are you coming in or staying out there for a wrestling match with Blackie?"

"We're going over to Percy's house," Mandy told her.

"We are?" James looked puzzled. "What for?"

"To take Twinkle out while Michael works," Mandy explained.

"Oh, right!" James said. "Blackie will love that. Do you think we could take Twinkle over to see Percy?"

"I could give you a ride over to Walton later if you like," Gran offered. "I've promised to visit a friend who's going away for Christmas."

"Thanks, Gran. That would be great," Mandy said. "What time shall we come back?"

Gran thought for a moment. "If you give me an hour, I'll have time to bake some cookies, too. I'll make enough for you to take some to Percy."

"OK. See you later." Then, following Gran's directions, Mandy and James set off for Percy's house, which was not far from Lilac Cottage. Blackie leaped beside them on his leash, jerking James's arm in its socket until James ordered him to calm down.

They had to knock on the door twice before Michael opened it. He came to the door wearing jeans and a sweater. "Hello again." He gave them a rather hasty grin and ran his hand through his hair. "Sorry. I was in the middle of a report."

"We thought you might be busy," Mandy said. "So we wondered if we could take Twinkle out for a walk and then to see Percy. Gran can give us a ride."

"We brought Blackie because he's really friendly and loves playing with other dogs," James added. "Twinkle would be doing us a favor if he could tire him out!"

"That's very thoughtful of you both. Thank you, that would be great." Michael patted Blackie's head. "Hello there, fella! He's a handsome dog, isn't he? Look, I don't mean to be rude, but I really must get back. . . ."

"That's OK. Shall I come in and get Twinkle?" Mandy asked.

Michael showed Mandy the way to the kitchen while James waited outside with Blackie. Twinkle was curled up in his bed, warm and snug beside the radiator. As soon as he saw her, he lifted his head and gave a short bark. He leaped up and trotted forward, his tail twirling around wildly.

"Hello, boy." Mandy bent down and gave Twinkle a cuddle, then clipped on his leash, which she found hanging beside the back door.

"See you later," she called out as she passed the living room.

Michael glanced up from his laptop. "Thanks very much, Mandy. You and James are real lifesavers! I'll tell Dad how helpful you've been when I go to see him later."

Blackie dashed across the field after Twinkle. Both dogs flew over the frozen ground, their paws making dark tracks in the frosty grass.

"Look at them go!" Mandy said.

Suddenly, Twinkle whipped around and came to a full stop. Blackie, being much heavier, shot past him and skidded to a clumsy halt. Then Twinkle gave a short bark and lunged forward. Blackie set off after him through the trees.

After a few minutes, both dogs trotted back. They were panting heavily, their breath steaming in the crisp air.

Mandy checked her watch. "We'd better start making our way back to Gran's. She'll be ready to leave by the time we get there. The dogs can have a drink before she gives us a ride to Walton."

James rubbed his gloved hands together. "And we can have a cookie!" he said appreciatively.

Mandy raised an eyebrow. "Or two or three, James Hunter!" She knew how much her friend loved Gran's cooking.

At Lilac Cottage the wonderful smell of baking filled every room. Blackie and Twinkle stretched out on the kitchen floor after their drink, both tired out after the exercise. Mandy and James munched on cookies, while Gran packed some of them into a box.

"I've put in a few extra so Percy can offer them around," she said. "Help yourself to another one, James."

"Thanks, Mrs. Hope. These are delicious." James wiped some crumbs from his mouth.

Mandy nudged him gently in the ribs. "Come on," she said. "If you eat any more, you'll burst. Let's get these dogs in the car before they fall asleep."

"You two better sit in the back with the dogs," Gran suggested. She carefully put the box of cookies on the passenger seat, then drove out onto the road.

Blackie and Twinkle behaved perfectly. They hung over the backseat, breathing hot doggy breath on Mandy and James. At the Walton hospital, Gran parked next to the entrance. Mandy and James climbed out and opened the rear door to let the dogs out.

"Can you manage this box?" Gran asked Mandy, eyeing Blackie and Twinkle, who were sniffing eagerly at the tempting baking smells. "I need to get going."

"Oh, yes." Mandy handed Twinkle's leash to James and took the box. "Thanks for the ride, Gran. See you later." Mandy waited while James took care of the two dogs. "I'll just take these cookies in for Percy," Mandy said.

"OK. Shall I take the dogs around to the window?" James suggested.

"Good idea," Mandy replied. "I'll come right back, and then we can hold Twinkle up for Percy to see." She made her way to Ward Twelve. Percy was sitting on his bed, wearing a bathrobe. He was talking to a familiar figure in yellow pajamas, sitting on a chair beside the bed.

"Hello, Percy. Hello, Charlie," said Mandy.

At the sound of her voice, they both looked up and smiled.

"Charlie's been keeping me company," Percy explained.

Mandy gave him the box of cookies. "These are a present from Gran," she said. "And you have another visitor outside. Twinkle! He's with James and Blackie. We'll hold him up for you to see in a minute."

A broad smile spread over Percy's face. "Oh, that's great, Mandy."

Charlie looked excited. "Can I see Twinkle, too? Mr. Green has been telling me all about terrier racing. And we bet Twinkle would be a champion racer, don't we?"

Percy nodded. "Charlie can't get enough of my stories. He's wearing me out with all his questions."

But Mandy could tell by his friendly grin that the old man was delighted to have someone to share his memories with. She looked at Charlie, who was leaning back in his chair and peering out the window, trying to get a glimpse of Twinkle. "We could bring him into Santaland before we go back to Welford," Mandy offered.

"Cool!" Charlie said.

Percy smiled at Mandy. "Good idea," he said. He turned to Charlie. "Why don't you go there and give Twinkle a hug from me? Tell him I'll see him soon."

"OK, I will," Charlie said delightedly. "See you there!" He marched through the ward, munching a cookie.

Mandy followed him. As she passed Santaland, she looked in and saw Charlie poking around among the piles of shiny wrapped presents. She smiled to herself.

James was looking a bit flushed. "I'm glad you're back. These two are a real handful!"

Blackie barked. He jumped up and put his front paws on the hospital wall. His nose was almost level with the windowsill. Twinkle did exactly the same, but his nose was a long way below the window.

"I think they both want to see Percy!" Mandy said. "Do you think we can manage that?"

"No problem!" James wrapped his arms around Blackie and managed to lift him just high enough to see into the window. Mandy scooped Twinkle up more easily.

Percy's face lit up with amazement when he saw both dogs. He smiled and waved. Twinkle pricked up his ears and yapped excitedly as soon as he spotted his owner. Mandy petted his head and held him close to her to stop him from wriggling out of her arms.

"Oof!" James's arms were aching. He put Blackie down. "That's all I can manage," he groaned.

Mandy waved at Percy, then put Twinkle down, too. "I told Charlie that we'd stop by Santaland with Twinkle," she said to James.

"Good idea," said James. "But I think I'll wait outside with Blackie."

Mandy nodded. Blackie running around a field was one thing, but putting the lively Labrador in an enclosed space with a table full of raffle prizes was another.

"Hello, Twinkle!" Charlie cuddled the little dog and kissed the top of his head. Twinkle whined softly and licked Charlie's ear. "Look! He remembers me!" Charlie beamed. "He's really smart, isn't he?"

Mandy smiled, her hands full of wrapped presents. There wasn't much left to do in Santaland now, although more gifts had been dropped off and Mandy was just adding them to the pile in front of the display boards.

She glanced at her watch. It was nearly one o'clock, and the bus back to Welford would be leaving soon. "I have to go now," she told Charlie. "I'll bring Twinkle back to see you again if it's OK with Michael." Charlie petted Twinkle once more and picked up the end of the leash. As he handed it to Mandy, she saw that he looked rather sad.

"Thanks for bringing him to see me," he said, managing to smile. Then he brightened up even more. "I'm all better now. I'm going home tomorrow," he told her proudly.

"That's great news," Mandy said, but she couldn't help noticing that Charlie's eyes never left Twinkle as she led the little dog out of the room. She wondered if Charlie was missing his friend already.

It was two o'clock by the time the bus reached Welford. Mandy and James got out at the Fox and Goose intersection, where the smell of food hung in the air.

James sniffed appreciatively. "Come on, Mandy," he said. "Let's take Twinkle home so that we can have our lunch."

Mandy rolled her eyes. "I can't believe you're hungry

after all those cookies!" she teased. But she called to Twinkle and followed James at a brisk pace along the road to Michael's house.

This time, Michael answered the door as soon as they knocked. "Hello again. Did you have a good time?"

"Oh, yes. Twinkle had a really long walk," said Mandy. "And Gran gave us a ride to the hospital so that Percy could see Twinkle again."

Michael smiled. "I bet Dad loved that! And I've just had some excellent news. The hospital phoned to say that Dad is making such good progress that he'll be coming home tomorrow."

"Oh, that's great!" said James.

Mandy handed Twinkle's leash to Michael. The Jack Russell pattered happily into the hallway, looking pleased to be home.

Michael bent down to pet the little dog. "I think this little guy has helped Dad get better. And you've really helped me, too. I've managed to get lots of work done today. Thanks very much."

"That's OK," Mandy said. "We enjoyed it — and so did Blackie."

Michael unclipped Twinkle's leash, then straightened up. "Dad's going to get a great surprise," he told them. "My wife and kids are on their way over from the States. We'll be staying with Dad until the New Year."

"Percy will love that," Mandy said. "And I'll let Gran know. I'm sure she'll have some spare cookies for you!"

Michael laughed. "That would be great!" he said, shutting the door.

As Mandy and James headed home, a few snowflakes began to fall. By the time they split up and went their separate ways, the flakes were as big as cotton balls, floating down and settling thickly on the icy ground. Blackie looked like a Dalmation in reverse, with big white snowflakes stuck to his shiny black coat.

"A white Christmas after all!" Mandy sang out happily as she turned toward Animal Ark.

Eight

"Laura should be coming in shortly to get Peaches, Mandy. Would you bring her back here when she arrives?" Dr. Emily stuck her head around the examination room door.

"OK," Mandy said. It was the last office hour before Christmas, and she was tidying the magazines in the waiting room. She had gone into the residential unit first thing to check on Peaches again. The guinea pig was lively and alert and ready to go home.

"Would you like to go in now?" Jean Knox sent in the next patient, a woman carrying a pet carrier with a large black cat inside. Then Jean smiled across at Mandy. "Just this patient for your mom to see, then we can all relax and have our Christmas."

Ten minutes later, the woman with the cat came out of the treatment room. She paused by the reception desk as Jean checked her computer, then peeled off a printed label and stuck it onto a small bottle. "One tablet to be given to Ebony twice a day for a week," she explained with a smile. The woman took the bottle and thanked Jean. "Now, do you need to make another appointment?" Jean asked, opening the appointment book.

Mandy glanced up at the clock and felt a tug of anxiety. Laura had better hurry up. It was almost lunchtime, and there were no afternoon office hours today.

Suddenly, Laura came dashing through the door, followed by her dad. She seemed close to tears. "Are we too late to pick up Peaches?" she burst out. "Our car wouldn't start because of the snow. But Dad finally managed to get it going."

Mandy smiled warmly. "Don't worry. You're just in time. I'll take you back, OK?"

"Phew!" Laura's dad shot Mandy a grateful glance. "That was close. Without Peaches, we would have had to cancel Christmas!"

"I'll go and get Peaches for you," Jean offered.

Mandy led the way into the examination room. While

they were waiting for Jean to bring Peaches, Dr. Emily gave Laura instructions about what to feed her pet from now on. "Remember, Laura. No plants from the cabbage family, like curly kale and cauliflower. But you can give Peaches small amounts of raw fruit and vegetables for a treat."

Mandy handed Laura one of the clinic's flyers about feeding pets. "This will remind you what she can have if you forget," she said.

"Thanks, Mandy," her mom said.

Laura had been listening carefully to Dr. Emily. "No cabbagey stuff," she repeated seriously. "What about parsley? It's Peaches's favorite."

Dr. Emily smiled. "Parsley's fine."

"Here we are." Jean came into the room and put a pet carrier onto the examination table.

"Peaches!" Laura exclaimed, opening the front of the carrier to pet her beautiful animal. "Oh, she looks a lot better. Her eyes are bright."

"That's because she's feeling well again," Mandy said. "I gave her a slice of apple this morning, and she dragged it straight into her nest to eat!"

Laura laughed. "She always does that. She must be feeling like her old self."

"She's recovered really well, considering her age," Dr. Emily agreed.

Laura petted Peaches gently. "Dad's built you a rack for the side of your hutch, so you won't step on your food," she whispered to her pet. Peaches looked up at her with beady black eyes and twitched her nose.

"It sounds like Peaches is going to get four-star treatment," Dr. Emily said.

"Well, we know what she's getting for Christmas dinner," Mandy joked. "Parsley!"

Laura picked Peaches up and placed her carefully in the cardboard pet carrier. Her dad carried it out of the examination room and stood at Jean's desk while he settled the bill. Then Mandy held the door for them and waved to Laura as she got into her dad's car. After they had left, Mandy helped lock up the clinic. Jean Knox put on her coat and scarf and picked up her handbag.

Mandy put her hand in the pocket of her jacket and took out a small, flat package. "Merry Christmas, Jean," she said.

"Oh, thank you, dear," Jean said, beaming. She took the parcel and popped it into her bag. "Merry Christmas to you, too. And you might find a little something from me under your Christmas tree!"

"That was kind of you," Dr. Emily said after Jean had gone. "What's in the package?"

"Oh, just a new chain for Jean's glasses," Mandy answered with a grin. "So she's got a spare in case she loses her other one!"

"Just time for lunch before I face my public!" Dr. Adam said, diving into a pile of sandwiches. He looked longingly at Gran's cookies.

"No time for dessert." Dr. Emily grinned at her husband. "Your Santaland is ready and waiting."

"Da-ad! You won't fit in your Santa suit if you keep on eating like that!" Mandy joked. Now that the last office hours were over, she was tingling with excitement. It felt as if Christmas had started already.

"But it's Christmas Eve!" her dad pointed out. He reached out and took a warm cookie. "Mmm. Yummy. I think I'll go and clear the driveway. Might work off that cookie!" He wiped his mouth and headed out the back door.

"I'll get your Santa suit," Mandy volunteered. She went into the living room, where the outfit was hanging, and carried the fake-fur-trimmed red suit into the kitchen.

Suddenly, a shout rang out. Mandy froze. That sounded like her dad's voice. She dashed out to the driveway. Dr. Adam had dropped the shovel onto the snow. Dr. Emily was there already, helping Mandy's dad move gingerly toward the house.

"What happened?" Mandy burst out.

Dr. Adam winced with pain. "It's my back," he groaned. "I slipped on a patch of ice — I think I've strained it."

"Oh, no! We're supposed to be leaving for the hospital in a minute," Mandy said.

"Your dad won't be going, I'm afraid," Dr. Emily said firmly. "He can't possibly be Santa now." She turned to her husband. "Remember when you strained your back before, Adam?"

"Yes," her husband murmured, rubbing his back. "I couldn't sit down for a week! I'm sorry, Mandy darling. I really hate to let everyone down. But I just can't do it."

Mandy's heart sank. She thought of all the children who were looking forward to visiting Santa. This was a total disaster!

Once they were all back in the kitchen, Dr. Emily took a bottle of painkillers out of the cupboard and filled a glass with water. Mandy's dad swallowed the pills, then limped out of the room, heading for the living room.

"I'm going to lie on the floor," he told them through clenched teeth.

Mandy sat down at the table and propped her chin on her hand. "Now what are we going to do?" she wailed.

Dr. Emily raised her eyebrows. "OK. Let's not panic. But we do need to find another Santa — and quickly!"

"What about Grandpa?" Mandy began. Then her face fell. "Oh, I just remembered. He's taking pies and Christmas cookies to Gran's meals-on-wheels people."

"That's right," her mom confirmed. "Your gran's at the hospital this afternoon, so she couldn't do it herself."

"There's no time left to ask anyone else, is there?" Mandy said glumly. She felt defeated. This was really awful.

"Maybe we could hand out the presents ourselves," Dr. Emily suggested.

"Mo-om!" Mandy looked at her mom aghast. "Not without Santa!" She stared out the kitchen window, racking her brain for a Santa substitute. Then she jumped up from the table. "Wait a minute. I just thought of someone who might do it. Come on!"

Snow blew thickly against the windshield as Dr. Emily drove the Land Rover carefully up the winding road across the moors. The fields and hedges were carpeted with a thick white blanket, and the snow formed smoky, wave-shaped drifts as the wind blew it against the walls.

As soon as they pulled into the hospital parking lot, Mandy jumped out and raced into the invitingly warm building. She was gasping for breath by the time she reached Ward Twelve. Gran was standing by Percy's bed. The old man was dressed in a thick coat and scarf and had a tweed cap on his head. It looked as though Percy was just about to go home.

Gran looked up in alarm as Mandy rushed to the bedside. "What's the matter? Has something happened?"

"It's Dad!" Mandy managed to gasp. "He's slipped and strained his back. He's OK, but he can't sit down, so he can't be Santa now. We need to find someone else to do it!"

"Oh, dear," Gran said. She glanced at her watch. "But it's too late. The children will start arriving in about twenty minutes."

"I know!" Mandy said. She took a deep breath. Would she be able to persuade Percy to step in? She remembered her gran saying that Percy was a very private person, but this was an emergency.

Percy was already taking off his cap and scarf. He unbuttoned his heavy outdoor coat. "I'll do it," he said. "Lead me to the Santa suit. I've heard so much about this Santaland, I'd love to see it."

"Oh, Percy! Thank you!" Mandy exclaimed. Without thinking, she stood on tiptoe and gave his wrinkled cheek a kiss. "The suit's still in the car. I'll go bring it in."

"Hold your horses a minute, Mandy dear," Gran interrupted. "Percy has been quite ill. This might be too much for him."

"Oh." Mandy hadn't thought of that. Her shoulders sagged.

But Percy spoke up. "Now, don't you worry about me. I feel fine," he protested.

Gran nodded, smiling. "I'm sure you do, Percy. But I think you should check with a doctor first, just to be on the safe side."

Percy winked at Mandy. "All right, Dorothy. If that will set your mind at rest."

"It would." Gran was unmoving.

Mandy's patience felt stretched to the limit. She knew that her gran was right, but there were only fifteen minutes left now before the visitors began arriving. She fidgeted anxiously as she watched the seconds tick past on her watch. Just then, Nurse Lacey entered the ward, followed by a tall blond man in a white coat.

"Here's the doctor now," said Gran.

"I'll go and have a word with him." Percy left his coat on the chair and went over.

Mandy waited tensely beside Gran. What were they going to do if the doctor decided that Percy ought to go straight home and rest?

Percy beamed as he came back over to Gran and Mandy. "I've got the all-clear! The doctor thinks being Santa is a great idea. Especially as I will be sitting down anyway for most of the time."

"Fantastic!" Mandy didn't need to be told twice. "I'll meet you and Gran over there!" She sped away to tell her mom the good news and get the Santa suit.

"Ho, ho, ho!" Percy had put on the Santa suit and was trying out his hearty Santa laugh. The suit was a bit long for him, but the rich red clothes looked very festive. He had even hooked Dr. Adam's fake white beard over his ears, although it tended to slip off if he moved his head too quickly.

Percy sat in a comfortable armchair borrowed from Nurse Lacey's office. Next to him a sack bulged with toys from the Christmas toy drive, all wrapped in brightly colored paper.

"You look great, Percy," Mandy told him.

"Very Christmassy," agreed Gran, putting a cushion behind Percy's back. "But you must stop at once if you feel tired, you hear?"

Percy grinned at Mandy. "Merry Christmas, everyone!" he boomed. His pale blue eyes sparkled, and his cheeks were a healthy pink above the thick white beard.

"Dad? Is that you?" said a surprised voice.

Mandy turned and saw that Michael had come into the room. Twinkle stood beside him, his ears pricked up and his head to one side as he studied the Santa figure.

"I've just been into the ward, and the nurse told me

you were in here," Michael said. "But I didn't expect this!"

"Hello, son. Come to visit Santa, have you?" Percy joked. "And what do *you* want for Christmas?"

Mandy chuckled. Percy was a great Santa.

"I've had my present, thanks," Michael said warmly. "My dad's going to be home and well for Christmas."

Mandy went over and gave Twinkle a cuddle. "Hello again, boy. Come to say hello to Percy, have you?"

Twinkle whined softly. He sat down and held up one paw, inviting Mandy to shake hands.

"Well," Percy said, "he's never done that before!"

"Charlie must have taught him," Mandy said.

Gran nodded. "That boy's been fantastic with Twinkle," she remarked.

Mandy took Twinkle's paw and gave it a gentle shake. "This is perfect!" she said. "We don't just have a new Santa, we have his honorary reindeer here, too!"

Twinkle gave a short bark, and his tail wagged crazily. He obviously agreed.

Nine

On the dot of three o'clock, children began coming into Santaland. Many of them were in hospital gowns and slippers, and some had nurses or parents accompanying them.

"Shall we get your reindeer dressed?" Mandy suggested to Percy.

"Excuse me? Oh, you mean the antlers Charlie made." Percy grinned. "He told me all about them. I can't wait to see Twinkle wearing them."

Mandy found the antlers behind the display boards and tied them on. Twinkle shook his head a couple of times, but he seemed pleased to be wearing his antlers again.

"There. You look great!" Mandy told him admiringly.

Just then James arrived. "Hi! Sorry I'm a bit late. The road across the moors is blocked, so we had to go through the valley." He glanced over to where Santa was surrounded by children. "Your dad's doing a great job," he said to Mandy.

"My dad?" Mandy laughed. "Look again!"

James peered across the crowded room. Santa was leaning down to listen as the children told him what they wanted for Christmas. His false beard had slipped to one side.

James frowned. "That's not your dad! It looks like . . ."

"Percy? Yes — it's him!" said Mandy. "Dad slipped on some ice and hurt his back, so Percy took over."

"And he's having the time of his life," Michael said. "I haven't seen Dad look this happy since the day I brought Twinkle home for him."

Mandy had to agree. The frail, depressed elderly man was gone, and now Percy looked cheerful and confident as he talked to his eager visitors.

Twinkle lay at Percy's feet, snuffling contentedly through a pile of loose tinsel. His antlers bobbed and wobbled as he dug his nose into the glittery strands, and he sneezed when they tickled his nose.

James nudged Mandy. "I think Twinkle's enjoying himself, too!" he said.

Mandy grinned. "A terrier in the tinsel! What a perfect Christmas present for Percy — he's going home and back to Twinkle." At the sound of his name, the Jack Russell looked up and barked, but he didn't move from Percy's feet.

Michael turned to Mandy and James. "Dad seems to be tied up for a while, so I'm going to slip out and do some last-minute shopping."

"OK," Mandy said. "We'll look after Twinkle. Don't worry."

"Oh, I almost forgot. Before I go . . ." Michael went and whispered something in Percy's ear.

Then Mandy saw him take a bulky wrapped package from his overcoat pocket and slip it into Santa's sack. Percy gave a secret smile and nodded at his son.

Strange, Mandy thought. *Who was that special gift for?*

"Cool! Twinkle's here!" Charlie bounded into the room wearing jeans, a thick sweater, and sneakers.

"Hi, Charlie," called James.

"I thought you were going home today," Mandy said.

"I am," Charlie replied promptly. "Mom's coming to get me. But I want to see Santa before I go. The nurse told me it's Percy! I have a present for him."

"What is it?" Mandy asked curiously.

But Charlie wasn't telling. "Wait and see!" he teased. While Charlie was waiting his turn, he went over to see Twinkle. Twinkle immediately rolled onto his back, inviting Charlie to pet his pale tummy. Charlie giggled and stroked him.

Santaland seemed to be getting even busier. The display boards swayed perilously as more children crowded in to see Santa. Mandy's grandmother was at the door taking money from the children who weren't hospitalized, and already her money basket was encouragingly full.

"You go and help Percy give out the presents," James suggested, "and I'll help your gran. That line out there is getting a little unruly!" He marched out of the room, and Mandy heard him asking the waiting children to line up on one side of the hall. Mandy wriggled through the people and made her way behind the raffle table, to Percy's side. She picked up a slippery armful of presents and got ready to hand them out.

It was Charlie's turn to see Santa. Mandy thought he looked rather shy all of a sudden. He was holding a long, tube-shaped gift.

Percy bent down and beamed through his beard. "Hello, young man," he said.

"Hello, Santa," Charlie answered. He thrust the present toward Percy. "This is for you."

"For me?" Percy sounded surprised. "What's all this,

eh? Santa's supposed to give you a present, not the other way around!"

"It's a special one. You can open it now," Charlie said seriously. "You don't have to wait until Christmas Day."

"In that case, I will!" Percy opened his present. It was a large, rolled-up sheet of paper. As Percy unrolled it, his eyes widened. "That's wonderful!" he exclaimed.

Mandy leaned over his shoulder to look. It was a portrait of Twinkle. The little dog was sitting in a heap of red tinsel, his head cocked to one side. One strand hung around his neck. Charlie had even captured the glint in the little dog's eyes.

"It's great!" Mandy gasped. "Really lifelike!"

"Did you draw that, Charlie?" James peered across the room and called over to them. "It's fantastic!"

"It certainly is," Percy echoed. "It's great, Charlie," he repeated. "Best present I've ever had!"

Charlie's face was bright pink, but he looked really pleased. Twinkle jumped up and pawed at Charlie's jeans. He barked as if in approval.

Percy grinned. "There you are. Twinkle agrees with me!" Percy rolled up the drawing again and stored it safely under his chair. Then he adjusted his false beard and smoothed down his red Santa suit. "Now it's your turn, Charlie. What would you like for Christmas?" he asked.

Charlie beamed. He leaned close and spoke quietly so that only Percy and Mandy could hear. "What I'd really like is my very own dog. Just like Twinkle."

Mandy felt a pang of sympathy. Since Charlie and his mom lived in an apartment and were out all day, she knew it just wasn't practical. There was no way he could have a pet dog.

Just then, Mandy heard a commotion in the hall. James appeared in the doorway, looking rather flustered.

"I can assure you, my dear, that my dogs are clean, healthy, and obedient!" The bossy voice floated into the Christmas room. "I can vouch for them personally."

Mandy raised her eyebrows at James. "Mrs. Ponsonby!"

"I'm afraid I'll have to get permission from the ward nurse before you bring in your dogs," one of the nurses was explaining patiently.

"But I'm Amelia Ponsonby from Bleakfell Hall," Mrs. Ponsonby interrupted. "Ah, here's someone who'll vouch for me. Dorothy dear, would you just . . ."

The conversation outside subsided into a murmur. James busied himself at the door, taking money from some waiting children. Mandy straightened the gifts on the raffle table.

A few moments later, Mrs. Ponsonby swept into the

room. She wore a fashionable purple coat and a matching woolen hat. Pandora was tucked under her arm, and Toby trotted on a leash by her side. Both dogs wore expensive little coats.

"Well, really! I only wanted to pop in for a few minutes," Mrs. Ponsonby blustered to Gran, who was behind her.

"It's hospital policy for everyone to get permission to bring in a dog, Amelia," Gran said hastily.

"You're probably right," Mrs. Ponsonby said as she surveyed the display. Her eyes flicked over the silver pillars, the walls with their tinsel streamers and stars, and Santa sitting on his comfortable armchair. "This is all splendid!" she boomed, looking up at Charlie's banner. "My, you have all worked hard." She marched over to the raffle table and started inspecting the prizes.

Toby trotted over to Twinkle. The two dogs sniffed each other curiously, their ears pricked. Then Toby bounced down low onto his front paws, inviting Twinkle to play. Twinkle leaped up and lunged forward, yapping playfully. Toby darted sideways, whipped around, and took off across the room.

Mandy laughed. Twinkle had completely forgotten that he was supposed to be an honorary reindeer! As he bowled into Toby, his antlers were knocked sideways and hung limply over his shoulder.

Toby sprang up and pretended to nip Twinkle's ear. Twinkle growled with mock fierceness and scampered behind Percy's armchair. His tiny claws clicked against the hard floor. In a second, Twinkle reappeared, trailing garland in his mouth. He shook his head, chewing it like a rat. Toby seemed very excited by the shiny stuff. He grabbed the other end of it and backed off, a growl rumbling cheerfully in his throat.

"Cool! A tug-of-war!" Charlie stood at the edge of the room and watched the dogs pulling the tinsel until it was stretched out between them.

Twinkle and Toby edged sideways, closer and closer to Mrs. Ponsonby. Then Toby leaped forward, still holding the garland. As Twinkle swerved away, the streamer became wound around the woman's sturdy ankles. It was pulled steadily tighter as the dogs dodged around her.

"Oh, my goodness! I can't move! Someone help me!" Mrs. Ponsonby boomed dramatically.

Mandy felt laughter bubbling up inside her as she ran over and grabbed Toby. Charlie managed to catch Twinkle and knelt down beside him, holding him still. The little dog looked up at him, panting, his pink tongue lolling out. He still seemed raring to go. James sprang forward and helped to unravel the garland from Mrs. Ponsonby's ankles.

Mrs. Ponsonby stamped her feet impatiently. "Do hurry and get it off, James dear! It's upsetting poor Pandora!"

Pandora blinked placidly, eyeing James calmly from her place in Mrs. Ponsonby's arms.

Keeping one hand on Toby's collar, Mandy rolled up the streamer. She stuffed it into her pocket so there'd be no chance of Twinkle running off with it again!

As soon as her feet were free, Mrs. Ponsonby clipped

Toby's leash on and swept out of the room in a flurry of purple coat and strong perfume. "I'll be back to see you later, Dorothy," she promised Mandy's gran threateningly. "When that disobedient terrier has left!"

"Oh, dear." Percy looked a bit worried. "Twinkle's a handful, isn't he? I hope he's not going to misbehave again."

"I'll look after him until Mom gets here, if you like," Charlie offered. He was still kneeling on the floor, petting Twinkle's back.

"Thanks, my boy," Percy said gratefully.

Twinkle looked up at Charlie, then put his chin on his front paws, as if he understood that the game was over.

"He really has a way with dogs, doesn't he?" Gran had been watching Charlie keep Twinkle under control.

"Yes," James agreed. "Twinkle and Charlie have really taken to each other." He took a donation from the last person in the line and led her to Santa's chair. Mandy took another toy out of Santa's sack and passed it to Percy. The little girl took it from Santa with a delighted grin and ran to show it to her mom, who was waiting by the door.

Mandy heaved a sigh of relief and propped herself on the edge of the raffle table. Galloping footsteps out in the hall made Mandy look up. Charlie was racing up and down, with Twinkle bounding at his heels, full of energy as usual. Then Mandy looked at Percy. The old man looked tired and a little pale, and his breathing sounded a bit noisy. Suddenly, the beginnings of a brilliant idea crept into Mandy's mind.

"Twinkle's so frisky and lively, isn't he?" she began. "It looks like you could use some help with him."

"Mandy's right, Percy," Gran agreed, coming over with the basket of money. "It's going to be some time before you're completely better. And as we've seen, Twinkle needs a lot of attention."

Percy's head came up. He looked a little uncomfortable. "Thanks, but I can manage," he said. "I don't want anyone coming to take Twinkle away because they think he's too much for me!"

Mandy's heart sank. Now Percy was upset. This wasn't what she wanted to happen. How on earth was she going to get him to agree to her perfect solution?

Ten

Mandy took a deep breath. She decided to try again. "Actually, Percy," she began carefully, "I was just thinking. What if Charlie helped you with Twinkle?"

Percy turned toward her. He still looked a bit uneasy. "How do you mean?"

"Well, you know how much Charlie loves dogs, especially Twinkle. And he can't have one of his own because he lives in an apartment and his mom works all day." Mandy rushed on, warming to her theme. James nodded eagerly to support her. "I bet he'd jump at the chance to come and take Twinkle for walks. And you would be making his dream come true if you let him see Twinkle sometimes." Mandy caught Gran's eye. She was looking rather stern. Mandy paused. Would Percy agree? He seemed so determined to be independent. James held his breath.

Suddenly, Percy's face cleared. "Oh," he said slowly. "So I'd still *keep* Twinkle. Charlie would just be helping me out."

"That's it!" said Mandy eagerly. "He could take Twinkle out for walks, and you'd be able to get better more quickly."

Percy looked thoughtful. "Well, I suppose we could try it," he said at last.

Just then, Charlie popped his head in the door. "Hi, Mandy!" he called. "Did you see how fast Twinkle can run?"

"Yes, I did," said Mandy. "And Charlie, Percy has just said that you can come and see Twinkle again, when he's at home."

Charlie's face lit up. He ran over to Percy's chair. "Can I, Mr. Green? Can I come and visit Twinkle and take him for walks?"

"Of course you can, my boy," Percy said, patting Charlie on the shoulder. "I'd like nothing better."

"Oh, that's great!" Charlie exclaimed.

Percy looked subdued for a moment. "To be honest, my legs aren't quite what they used to be. I'm not really up to taking Twinkle for a good long walk every day."

"But I am!" Charlie told him happily. "And you can tell me more about dog breeding and terrier racing, too. Because I'm definitely going to work with dogs when I grow up."

Percy chuckled at Charlie's enthusiasm. "I bet you will, too. I was dog crazy just like you when I was a kid!"

Charlie bent down and wrapped his arms around Twinkle. The little dog jumped up and balanced his front paws on Charlie's knee. Then he reached up and licked his face. "We're going to have such fun together, Twinkle," Charlie promised. "Just wait until I tell Mom about you."

"I'm afraid I've heard enough, Charlie," said a voice behind them.

Mandy and James turned around to see Linda Kingston. She had come to take Charlie home and was holding her son's outdoor clothes over her arm.

"Hi, Mrs. Kingston," Mandy said. She hopped down from the table and walked across to greet her.

But Linda Kingston was looking down at Charlie cuddling Twinkle. Her mouth was set in a stern line. "Now, Charlie," she said firmly, "I've told you that you can't have a dog. It's no use trying to persuade me once again."

James and Mandy glanced at each other in alarm.

"But I'm not, Mom!" Charlie interrupted, looking hurt. "I know you're going to love Twinkle."

"That's enough, Charlie!" Mrs. Kingston said in an annoyed voice. She looked at Mandy and James and frowned. "I'm afraid you really must not encourage Charlie to think he can have a dog. Especially when I've explained the situation to you both."

"But we haven't, have we, James?" Mandy said hurriedly, blushing.

James shook his head vigorously. "Charlie doesn't want to keep Twinkle," he explained. "He just wants to help Percy look after him."

Mrs. Kingston looked at Charlie. "Is this true?" she asked, her face clearing.

Charlie rolled his eyes. "Yes! That's what I've been trying to tell you! Twinkle is still Percy's dog, not mine!"

Then Percy spoke up. "You've got a fine boy there, Mrs. Kingston. He's been marvelous with my Twinkle these past few days. He's really cheered me up, I can tell you. And he drew me a wonderful picture of Twinkle for Christmas. He's offered to come and take him for walks to save my old legs. You should be proud of him."

Mandy and James exchanged hopeful glances.

Mrs. Kingston looked at Charlie and Percy, then down at Twinkle. "Oh, dear. I've been jumping to conclusions, haven't I?" She turned to Mandy and James. "I think I owe you both an apology."

"That's all right," Mandy said quickly.

"So — you don't mind me helping out with Twinkle?" Charlie said to his mom.

Mrs. Kingston shook her head. "Mind? I think it's wonderful!" She put a hand on her son's shoulder. "The doctor said you needed to get plenty of fresh air and exercise. And I can't imagine that a little dog like that is going to tire you out much."

Mandy opened her mouth to protest, but James nudged her and she shut it again. Out of the corner of her eye, she saw Percy wink at her.

Charlie beamed. He gave Twinkle another cuddle. "I'm going to come and take you out every day after school," he whispered into his soft brown ear. "And during school vacations we can go for super-long walks over the fields. This is the best Christmas present I've ever had!"

Percy chuckled. "Well, I *am* Santa, after all!" he declared, his blue eyes twinkling.

It was time for Santa to do a tour of the children's ward. He was going to meet the children who were too sick to leave their beds and visit Santaland. Mandy was a little worried that Percy would be tired by now, but he insisted he felt fine. Gran brought him a cup of tea and encouraged him to rest while they packed up the presents.

"There have been so many donations of toys this year," Mandy said, picking up a bulging sack.

"I think some people came back twice, just to see Twinkle!" James joked.

Nurse Lacey had given permission for Twinkle to make the rounds with Percy. His antlers were fixed firmly in place. Before he went home with his mom, Charlie had wound a strip of tinsel around Twinkle's collar. The terrier looked very festive and trotted eagerly around their feet, sniffing at the sacks of presents.

Mandy and James each shouldered a sack of toys. To make them look more Christmassy, Gran had produced two elves' hats made of green felt, with a bell on the pointed end. Mandy hoped they weren't going to pass any mirrors. She didn't think James would keep his hat on if he knew how funny he looked!

"Everyone ready? Let's go!" Percy started forward, followed by his honorary reindeer and two elf helpers.

Just before they entered the children's ward, James made them all stop. "Hang on a minute, everyone!" he said. "I nearly forgot." He delved into his trouser pocket and produced a CD. Dashing across to the ward nurse,

he asked her if she would play it for them. Then he hurried back to join Mandy, Percy, and Twinkle. "OK!" he
said. "We're ready!"

"What's on the CD?" Mandy asked.

"Oh, just Christmas carols," James replied. Then he
lowered his voice. "And there's a surprise at the end for
Percy," he whispered.

As Santa stepped through the doorway into the ward,
the strains of "Hark! the Herald Angels Sing" rang out.

"Ho, ho, ho! Merry Christmas, everyone!" Percy's
cheery voice filled the ward.

Twinkle trotted along beside Percy, his head held
high and his tail wagging furiously. His glittery tinsel
collar shone, and his antlers stood up perkily. He gave a
couple of excited barks.

"I think he's saying Merry Christmas, too!" Mandy said.

"Oh, look at that funny dog!" said a little boy in a blue
bathrobe. He wriggled to the end of his bed for a closer
look.

"Isn't he gorgeous!" agreed his mom. She reached
down and petted Twinkle, who had come up to say
hello.

Percy sat down at the bedside of a pale little girl who
looked about six years old. Her mom and dad sat with
her. Mandy hovered at the end of the bed, carrying the
sack of presents.

"Hello there. Merry Christmas! And what's your name?" Percy asked in a friendly voice.

"Fiona," the little girl told him shyly. She was propped up against a bank of pillows. "Is that your dog?" she asked, leaning over to look at Twinkle, who had scampered across the ward to join them.

Percy nodded. "He's my special helper. He's named Twinkle."

"May I pet him?" asked the little girl.

"Of course you may," said Mandy. She put down her sack and lifted Twinkle up so that Fiona could reach him. Fiona's parents looked a bit concerned, as if they thought Twinkle might be too lively for their sick daughter.

But Twinkle snuggled down in Mandy's arms and whined softly in a friendly fashion while he was petted. The little girl's face lit up, and she beamed proudly at her mom and dad as Twinkle nudged his head against her hand, asking for more attention. Percy took a pink-wrapped gift from the sack and laid it on the bed.

More Christmas carols rang out as they moved down the ward. Now it was "Deck the Halls."

Most of the other children were just as eager as Fiona was to make a fuss over the little dog. Mandy and James took turns picking Twinkle up and holding him while his ears were ruffled and his coat was petted again and again.

Twinkle behaved perfectly. He didn't even seem to mind when one of the children bent down and whispered into his ear.

"That must tickle!" Mandy said to James.

"He seems to know he has to be gentle, doesn't he?" James answered.

Percy was a great Santa. He spoke to every child, giving them presents and asking them what they wanted for Christmas. Mandy felt proud as she watched the children excitedly opening their presents.

"Wow! A giant book of animal stories!" A boy with his leg in a cast showed his present to his smiling parents.

At last, every patient had been visited. Santa waved as he began to make his way back through the ward. "Good-bye, everyone. Have a wonderful Christmas!" Percy called.

The last carol ended. There was a pause, then a familiar tune started up. "Twinkle, Twinkle, Little Star!"

"It's Twinkle's song!" Mandy said with a laugh. So *that* was James's surprise.

Percy beamed and walked slowly out of the ward with Twinkle bouncing at his heels. He led the way back to Santaland, where they began to clean up. The ice cave had started to look worn, and there were stray pieces of tinsel and torn wrapping paper everywhere.

"Oh, what's this?" Mandy shook her sack. "There's something left in the bottom."

Percy reached into the sack and took out a wrapped gift. He smiled at James. "I think this is for you."

"It can't be." James looked blank as he took hold of the parcel. "I'm not in the hospital."

"It has your name on the gift tag," Percy insisted.

"To Blackie, care of James Hunter. Best wishes from

Twinkle," James read aloud. He looked at Mandy. "Do you know what it is?"

Mandy shook her head. "Why don't you open it and find out?" she suggested. She watched curiously as James tore open the wrapper.

He looked into the package, and let out a burst of laughter. He grinned at Mandy and held up a doggy Christmas stocking.

"That's to replace the one you donated to Twinkle!" Percy told him.

The stocking was enormous, even bigger than the one Twinkle had eaten. There were bags of dog treats, dog chews, dog shampoo, and even a nifty collar.

"It's fantastic. Blackie's going to love this," James said happily. "Thank you, Percy."

Mandy smiled to herself. So that's what Michael had been whispering to his dad about!

Just then, Nurse Lacey popped her head around the door and offered them the use of her office so that Percy could take off his Santa suit. Mandy and James went with him to give him a hand. The old man seemed tired, but Mandy could see that he was glowing with happiness.

"Thanks so much, Percy. You were a wonderful Santa," she said to him.

Percy smiled at her. "I really enjoyed myself, Mandy. And so did Twinkle!"

As if in response, Twinkle gave a short, answering bark.

"I think Twinkle was even more popular than Santa!" James joked.

"And he should be!" Percy grinned. That was fine by him. He was very proud of his smart, friendly dog.

Suddenly, a group of people appeared at the doorway. "Surprise!"

It was Michael, with his wife and two small children, just in from the States. Twinkle raced over to meet them, his tail wagging crazily.

Percy stood stock-still. His tired face lit up with a huge smile. "Well, I never," he said delightedly.

"Merry Christmas, Grandpa!" said his family.

"Come on, let's leave them to themselves," Mandy whispered to James. "Gran will be waiting for us."

They crept out of Nurse Lacey's office and took one last look at the excited scene. Percy was sitting down, an arm around each of his grandchildren. Twinkle stood beside him. His front paws were on Percy's knees, and he was licking anyone who came within reach.

Mandy smiled. "That's the best present," she said to James. "Percy has all his family with him for Christmas."

   "And don't forget Charlie's going to help with Twin-kle," James reminded her. "I bet he can't wait to see him again!"

   "That's right," said Mandy. "Twinkle's been a real Santa's helper this year!"